SEASONS REMEMBERED

A TIME TO KEEP

Linda Shands

INTERVARSITY PRESS
DOWNERS GROVE, ILLINOIS 60515

InterVarsity Press® is the book-publishing division of InterVarsity Christian Fellowship®, a
student movement active on campus at hundreds of universities, colleges and schools of nursing in
the United States of America, and a member movement of the International Fellowship of
Evangelical Students. For information about local and regional activities, write Public Relations
Dept., InterVarsity Christian Fellowship, 6400 Schroeder Rd., P.O. Box 7895, Madison, WI
53707-7895.

Cover illustration: David Darrow
ISBN 0-8308-1931-2

Printed in the United States of America ∞

Library of Congress Cataloging-in-Publication Data

Shands, Linda, 1944-
    A time to keep/Linda Shands.
      p.   cm.—(Seasons remembered)
    ISBN 0-8308-1931-2 (alk. paper)
    I. Title.   II. Series: Shands, Linda, 1944-   Seasons remembered.
  PS3569.H329T56   1994
  813'.54—dc20   94-28135
                                                                     CIP

17	16	15	14	13	12	11	10	9	8	7	6	5	4	3	2	1
08	07	06	05	04	03	02	01	00	99	98	97	96	95	94		

To Mama
with Love

Prologue

Look at her primping by the mirror, swishing her skirt from side to side and smoothing out her curls. Sometimes when she tilts her head just so and flings her auburn hair back over her shoulder she looks so much like Mama I could cry.

It scares me too, a little. She wants to fly, that girl. But she's only thirteen. She should still be curled up in a snug warm nest, not prancing around anxious to spread her wings.

Liberty Jane; my Libby. She's bigger than I was at her age, taller, and has more bosom. Why, Aunt Rose said to me the other day, "Cissy, you need to get that child some support. She's getting much too big for undershirts."

Aunt Rose still calls me Cissy, although she's about the only one. My given name is Celia, but Papa nicknamed me Cissy when I was just a few months old and I guess it stuck. Grandma Eva didn't like it; she called me Celia up until the day she died, but everyone else called me Cissy for a long, long time. When I went back to using Celia, Aunt Rose sighed and said, "You'll always be Cissy to me," and I've never tried to change her mind.

Dear Aunt Rose. After her comment about the undershirts, I started watching and saw the signs of Libby growing up. She

moons around and dreams a lot—like she's doing now. I should
tell her to take her dreams to bed, but I hate to spoil her evening. I just wish her head was full of paper dolls and school
friends and what she's going to wear to church next Sunday.
But I'm afraid there's a young man dancing in there too.

Sometimes I don't think I can handle it. Libby growing up,
I mean. Maybe it would be different if I'd done my own growing
up with the family I was born to. Aunt Rose is sweet as pie,
I love her dearly, but she doesn't know much about the world.
Not like Mama did. Of course, Mama knew almost too much.
Papa too. I cried today and came close to cursing both of them.
I had to get down on my knees and ask forgiveness for my
anger. I haven't thought about it all in years. If it hadn't been
that Libby needed a dress for her first real party, I wouldn't
have thought about it now.

I'd made her two new dresses for Christmas but she insisted
they wouldn't do. "They're too plain, Mother," she wailed. "I
need something nice."

I was at a loss. We couldn't afford to buy something new and
there wasn't time to shop for material.

Then I remembered the dress. "It's blue," I told her, "periwinkle blue to match your eyes."

Libby steadied the chair while I climbed into the attic. There
wasn't much up there. Two or three boxes of books and bric-
a-brac, and one box marked CELIA MARIE SUMMERS 1936.
I handed it down, and by the time I had eased myself down out
of the hole and shut the trap door, Libby had the box dusted
off and opened.

"What's this?" she asked, holding up a small red book.

The golden clasp caught a beam of sunlight from the open
window and reflected it against the glass in the dresser mirror.
My hand stopped brushing dirt from my cheeks and reached
across a span of more than twenty years.

"Mom, what's wrong?" I heard the worry in her voice as I gently drew the book from her grasp.

I took a deep breath to quiet my spirit. I hadn't expected the cold hard knot of pain.

"Mom?" Libby sounded scared.

I pulled myself together. "It's a diary, hon. My diary from a long time ago."

"A diary from when you were young? Can I see?"

I let my hand slide across the smooth, red cardboard to the clasp that wrapped around the side and snapped on top. "Not now, Libby. It's locked, and I don't have the key." Why did I lie? I knew very well where the key was. "Anyway, we have to get to the dress. It will surely need pressing and maybe alterations." I slipped the diary into my pocket and bent down to dig through the box. The look on Libby's face when she saw the dress almost broke my heart.

"Mom!" she cried, tears already puddled in her eyes. "I can't wear that. It's all ruffles and frills. And look at the sash. No one wears this kind of thing anymore."

I wanted to give her a swat. Instead I pulled the rest of the tissue from around the dress and shook it out. I walked to the window and held it up in the light.

"It won't be so bad," I said, forcing myself to sound cheerful. "We'll fix it so it fits just right, and I have a ribbon that will work in place of the sash."

Libby didn't look convinced so I put on my no-nonsense face. "Anyway, young lady, there's no other choice. Not on this short notice. It's either this dress or something you already have." I spread the dress out on the bed and patted Libby's hand. "You decide, sugar. If you want to try the dress, we'll work on it tonight after dinner."

That was yesterday. Now look at her grinning at the mirror. She was the hit of the party.

I was fourteen when I wore that dress. It goes so well with her freckled skin, auburn hair and glowing eyes. Fits her better than it ever did me.

Meanwhile I spent the hours she was at the party looking through my diary. Not that there's much to it. I wrote in fragments then, bits and pieces really, but enough to spark a lifetime of memories.

Chapter
One

Things were good up till September 1933. I had just turned eleven, and I remember sitting on the wide front porch of our house in Pike, Nevada. I held Chuckie on one knee and snapped green beans into Mama's deep red porcelain bowl. Krista had her doll Samantha underneath the maple tree. They were having a tea party, and every once in a while she'd bring me a pretend cup to taste. Chuckie just gurgled and drooled on the green beans.

It was early afternoon, long time to go till supper, when I saw a cloud of dust coming down the side road. When it cleared away enough to see, I knew it for Papa's big old Nash, rolling over rocks and chuckholes, coming fast enough to beat the band. It kicked up dust all over Mrs. Wilson's laundry. Boy, was she going to be mad!

"Mama, Papa's coming." I picked up Chuckie and started for the door but Mama was already there, wringing her hands into a red-and-white checked dishtowel, her face all quiet and blank, like an empty chalkboard on a Monday morning.

Right then I knew something might be wrong. First off, Papa never came home before dark time. Never. "I may only be a clerk, but I always stay until the last dog is hung." That's how he put it. Then there was Mama's face. She was usually all smiles when Papa came home. Ready for a hug and kiss and to hear about his day. She had a thing for Papa, Mama did. I knew it even then and I'd just turned eleven.

Anyway, when I saw Mama's face so still and her hands all twisted up in that towel, I knew something could be wrong and felt sort of cold all over. Like when you get the flu on a hot summer day and should be burning up, but instead you feel chilled to the bone and ask Mama for the heavy goose-down quilt. That kind of cold.

"Cissy, go put Chuckie in his crib," Mama whispered, "and set the table while you're in there." Her voice was low, but I heard and started for the door.

"Take Krista with you." It was her do-it-now-and-don't-ask-questions tone.

I grabbed Krista from the stair rail, where she had climbed to watch Papa's car clattering up the road, and dragged her and Chuckie into the house.

Chuckie started to cry when I put him in his crib, and Krista tried to run back out the door. I was busy for a minute or two until I got them settled down, Chuckie with a bottle of juice and Krista with a pencil and the back of an old envelope. She loved to play at writing, Krista did. She was only five, but she could print her name and count to ten. She was Papa's little jewel. Red-gold hair that sort of sparked in the sun. Sweet and soft and ladylike, even in her old blue gingham play dress. Why, she could charm a candy from Papa's pocket just before supper time!

I heard the Nash chug up the drive and the heavy door slam shut, just like it did every night come seven or eight o'clock. Only now it was nearer four and Papa wasn't laughing or calling for his Pumpkins like he always did. We were all his Pumpkins, Chuckie and Krista and me. "Found you in the pumpkin patch," he'd say, "and you were all so plump and pretty we decided to keep you."

"Forever, Papa?" I would ask.

"Forever," he would promise and shake his head for yes with his serious bank-clerk look.

"Cross your heart?" Krista would ask, and he would kiss her cheek and ruffle Chuckie's damp blond curls and smile at Mama and tell us all about his day.

The front door opened and shut again. Mama and Papa whispered in the living room, then went to their bedroom and shut the door. I knew better than to bother them in there, so I tried to pretend I didn't know something could be wrong and set the table.

Five o'clock came, then six. I changed Chuckie, fed him mashed potatoes and gave him a bottle of milk. Krista had finished drawing a kitty, our house and her doll Samantha, all on the back of one envelope. She started to cry for Mama, so I fed her too and bribed her into bed with a lollipop.

Seven o'clock. Papa came out of the bedroom and left the house. I heard the rattle, chug, thunk of the Nash backing down the drive. Mama's face stayed quiet all night long. Red and puffy too.

"We'll talk about it in the morning," she told me. "Did you eat yet?" I nodded yes and she said, "You're a good girl, Cissy. Now brush your teeth and say your prayers and go to bed." I wasn't happy about it but I went. I hated to see Mama cry. I lay and worried maybe someone's dead. I almost got up to ask, but thought better of it.

I guess I must have gone to sleep because I didn't hear Papa come home. I felt him tuck me in, though, and brush his hand through my hair like he always did. Maybe everything was all right now—even if his breath on my cheek smelled funny. Like Jimmy Wilson's crazy Uncle Harry when he came to town from the railroad yard. I should have prayed right then. Maybe if I had prayed things would have turned out different.

I remember waking up the next morning and getting ready to go to school. My green plaid dress was dirty, so I buttoned up my old gray and tied my red silk scarf over the stain on the bodice. Papa had given me the scarf for Christmas. I never wore it except for good, but today I figured it would be okay since Mama hadn't had time to do the wash.

I combed my hair straight back and tied it at the neck and bottom with two strips of rag. Papa thought my hair was beautiful. "The color of September wheat," he said. "Don't ever cut that child's hair, Lynetta," he warned my mother. "It's her crowning glory." I had learned a long time ago to never braid it. Not for school anyway. Braids were just too tempting for the boys. Jimmy Wilson could sure yank hard, and then I'd yell and we'd both get in trouble and next time he'd yank even harder to pay me back. It was easier just to wear it long and loose or tie it with a rag.

By the time I did my teeth and went out for breakfast, Chuckie should have been sitting in his high seat, all pink and clean and happy, chewing on a piece of toast and slopping milk all over the floor. Krista should have been washed and dressed for play. Instead I found them both in the middle of the living room floor, eating corn flakes from the box, smelling like two-week-old laundry.

Mama came out of her room just then. She looked tired and old and sad, sort of like she did when Grandma Eva passed away. I thought again how someone must have died, but I couldn't figure who. Both grandmas and grandpas had passed on long before. We didn't have anyone else.

Before I could ask her, though, Mama hugged me quiet like and said so soft I could hardly hear, "Cissy, could you stay home from school today and watch the little ones? Papa and I have some things to take care of in town."

I swallowed a lump and nodded yes. I wanted to go to school, but what else could I do? We were practicing for a Christmas play and I really wanted the part of Mary, Jesus' mother. I'd make a good Mary, I was sure of it. Mrs. Greenwood thought so too and she was going to let me try it out.

Oh well, I thought, I'll just stay home and practice on Chuckie. Baby Jesus could have never been as dirty as Chuckie was then! Cereal and grape-juice stains all over his pajamas. Diaper leaking too. I could smell it.

By the time I had the others bathed and fed it was too late to go to school anyway. Papa came out of the bedroom. He looked different than before, funny somehow, like he was ashamed. He smiled at me and rubbed Krista's cheek but didn't talk to any of us, just nodded at Mama and went to start the car. Mama had washed her face and put on lipstick. "Your smile's crooked, Mama," Krista said, tilting her head for a kiss.

Mama just patted her hair. "Don't go off now," she said, and followed Papa out the door.

They didn't come back till after dark. By then I had washed the clothes, fed the kids some green beans and put them both to bed. When I told Krista to go to sleep, she cried for Mama. I didn't smack her but I wanted to. I felt all mean inside.

When Mama and Papa walked through the door, I acted like a brat and yelled at them for leaving me with all the work. I said bad things about how they didn't love me anymore, and if I was old enough to take care of the babies, I was old enough to know what was going on.

Afterward I thought how Mama should have flipped my lip for sassing. But she didn't.

Chapter
Two

If I close my eyes I can smell the jasmine blooming sweet and heady by the front porch. It bloomed that night and many nights after when I sat there on the step and tried to think what could I do to make things better.

I knew the word *Depression,* but it was a word for other folk, not us. We prayed for them at church and school, the ones who lost their money and their jobs. We prayed that they'd find food, and we brought hand-me-down clothes.

But Papa had a job. A good job too, working for a bank in town. We always had enough to eat and clothes to wear. We even got a radio that year. What a lark that was! So big it took up most of the floor space between the window and Papa's chair. It was dark brown wood and ran on batteries. There were big brown pads connected to a wire that you put over your ears to hear the most wondrous things! The New York Philharmonic and a funny show called "Amos and Andy." It was mostly Papa's radio, of course, but Mama and I took turns listening, and later when Mr. Roosevelt was elected president of the country, Papa told us everything they said about him on the radio.

"Oh, Cissy," Mama said that night after I yelled at them and was mean, "we didn't mean to hurt your feelings."

She looked at Papa. He shrugged and stared out the window, even though it was so dark you couldn't see the toad, let alone the wart on its nose.

"Papa lost his job, Cissy." Mama bent and hugged my shoulders tight. "The bank went under. So many are, these days." She sighed and set her hat and gloves on top of the radio. "But don't you worry, he'll find another job. Won't you, Charles? And everything will be just fine. The good Lord will provide. He always does."

Mama smiled and touched my hair.

"Tell the child the truth, Lynetta!" Papa turned away from the window and looked me straight in the eye. "Times are hard for everyone, Cissy. If I don't find work soon, we'll have to let the house go. We'll have to move. Now, we need you to be a brave, good girl and help with the chores because your Mama isn't feeling well."

He turned and went into the bedroom then. But before he shut the door he said, "I love you, Pumpkin. You know I do."

I heard him, but my mind was still fussing with what he had said about losing the house. I didn't like that. I didn't want to move. I wanted to stay right there—in my school, with my friends. I wanted to be baby Jesus' mother, Mary, in the Christmas play.

Now all of a sudden there was so much to think about. Mama had been feeling sick since July. She threw up every day. Slept a lot too. When she started sewing tiny things from one of her old flannel nightgowns, I knew Chuckie would not be the baby much longer. With Mama sick, I had to help out with the little ones, and soon there'd be another. It made me tired just to think of it.

Papa tried. He got up every morning and went into town. He came home in the afternoon with funny breath and a tired smile. He laughed and joked and ruffled Krista's hair, but I could tell he didn't really mean it.

Jimmy Wilson couldn't play with me anymore. Mr. and Mrs. Wilson said how it was all Papa's fault that they were poor and all their life savings had crashed with the bank. Didn't they know we were poor now too? Mama needed medicine and Chuckie needed shoes.

And I needed a costume for the school play!

I jumped up and down the day Mrs. Greenwood said I got the part. I stomped all over my new yellow pencil and broke the lead, but I didn't care. I was going to be Jesus' mother, Mary! It was only October but I already knew my lines; all I needed was a costume to wear. Mrs. Greenwood said not to worry. "If your mother can't make you an outfit, I'll try to find something in the donation bag for you to use."

That almost ruined the fun for me. Donations were for other folk, not us. And anyway, God would provide. Mama said so.

I ran the last six blocks from the bus stop to the mailbox. Then I straightened my skirt and pulled up my socks and smoothed back my hair. Mama wanted me to be a little lady. Today it was important for me to try.

"Mama?" I knocked softly on the bedroom door. Chuckie was in his crib, sound asleep. I could hear Krista in there talking to Samantha, so I opened the door. Mama lay real quiet. Her eyes were open so I knew she was awake, but she just stared at the wall like I wasn't even there.

Krista ran up to me and handed me Samantha. "Samantha fell down, Cissy. Will you kiss her and make it better?" I kissed the pretend sore on Samantha's knee and promised Krista her dolly would feel better soon. That was more than I could say for Mama. She tried to smile when I touched her shoulder, but I knew that she felt sick again. I figured it wasn't a good time to ask about a costume, so I took Krista into the kitchen and made Samantha some pretend tea.

* * *

Chuckie got the scarlet fever that winter. Papa had a job for a while. Doing the accounting books for the *Pike Review*. Everybody still took the paper. Well, almost everybody. Susi Cummings's older brother left home to find a job and never sent back money, so they couldn't even buy the Sunday funnies. But Susi's father said it didn't matter; there was only bad news anyway and who wanted to read about the banks collapsing, and people getting poor, and homeless families living in leaky tents, and garbage dumps on the way to California.

When Chuckie got sick Doctor Fix put a sign on our front door. It read QUARANTINE. "That means no one can come in or go out until he's well," he said. "How about that, Cissy— no school for a while!" The doctor winked and patted me on the head like I'd be happy about that, then he marched right on out the door slick as you please. *If scarlet fever is all that contagious,* I wondered, *why'd he get to leave?*

Papa was at work the day the doctor came. Our telephone had been cut off the month before so Mama couldn't call and tell him to not come home. Anyway, where else could he go?

It was Mama's idea to use the paper. Papa snuck around the back and hid on the mud porch, and Mama and I taped newspaper over the windows so no one could see in. He stayed there on the mud porch for two weeks, sleeping on an old army cot and eating on top of, really on the bottom of, the upturned washtub. We kept the door shut and Mama wore a paper mask so she wouldn't pass on germs. Papa had to sneak in and out to go to work. If Mrs. Wilson ever saw, she didn't tell. Maybe she forgave him for the bank collapsing after all.

Those were the longest two weeks of my life. We missed church three Sundays in a row. I couldn't go to school, and the Christmas play was only three weeks away. No one knew how long Chuckie would be sick. Or if Krista or I would get sick too.

I worried so hard. I prayed every night for Jesus to make Chuckie well. Mama looked tired and pale. Her shiny brown hair got streaks of white. But she wouldn't let me help nurse Chuckie. "We can't have you sick too," she said when I tried to take Chuckie some soup. "Why don't you read Krista a story? It will keep her out from under my feet."

So Mama took care of Chuckie, and Papa went to work, and I took care of Krista and worried a lot 'cause I still didn't have a costume and the play was only three weeks away.

I prayed about that too. I promised Jesus that if he got me a costume I would act like a little lady and not complain about extra chores around the house. I even promised to not throw mudballs at Jimmy Wilson, but I guess a lady wouldn't throw mudballs anyway, so that promise didn't count.

Two days later Chuckie got better, and I went looking for the ornaments.

Chapter
Three

With Chuckie better, Mama decided we would have Christmas after all. She asked me to find the Christmas tree ornaments. They were in a box on the rafters in a corner of the garage. Papa wasn't home and she didn't want to waste one more minute, there was too much to do.

I explained about my promise to be a little lady, and how ladies couldn't put on overalls and crawl around the rafters in a dirty garage. Mama just smiled and said how it would be okay just this once. "Pretend you're on a mission of mercy," she said. "People on a mission of mercy sometimes have to wear overalls and get dirty. You want Chuckie and Krista to have a good Christmas, don't you?"

Well, I had to agree with that, so I slipped on Papa's old painting overalls and rolled up the pant legs and sleeves.

The garage was out back, in the corner of the yard where a chicken coop used to be. It was dark and cold inside and smelled like rotten leaves. I had to stand in the doorway awhile before I could make out the rafters and find the box. There were three boxes. They were all more or less in the same place, so I hitched up my pant legs and boosted myself to the workbench and from there to the nearest bare rafter. It wasn't any harder than climbing the old willow in our backyard, and I'd been doing that since I was six.

I inched along till I could see into the first box. A small brown spider crawled over the edge and spun a web all the way to the ground. I don't like spiders the way Mrs. Wilson doesn't like snakes. I saw her chop a garden snake in half with the hoe one day. "The only good snake is a dead one," she hollered and threw the poor thing in the huckleberry bushes by the road, both ends still wiggling to beat the band. That's how I feel about spiders but I let this one live. I figured it wasn't right to kill anything when you're on a mission of mercy.

The curtains were in the second box. They were supposed to be white, but they'd yellowed some from the dirt and the weather and all. Now they were a creamy color, trimmed in pale blue. Mama said later they were real linen and used to belong to Grandma Eva before she passed on.

It occurred to me I'd found my costume, but I was afraid to shake them out right then. When there's one spider there could be more, and a person can only take so much. So I dropped them—box and all—to the dirt below and scooted along the beam to the last box. The ornaments were there but I couldn't reach the workbench without dropping the box. And I couldn't drop it: the pretty glass balls with the painted figures would surely break. Mama loved that set of ornaments. "Cherish them," she said. I didn't know what *cherish* meant, but I knew they meant a lot to her and I didn't want anything to happen to them. Each glass ball had a different nativity figure painted on the front. Mary, Joseph, baby Jesus. There were three wise men, two shepherds, a donkey and a lamb. Each one tied on top with a piece of colored lace.

I wasn't sure what to do. So I just sat there in Papa's too-big overalls, legs straddling the dusty rafters, and kept my eyes peeled for spiders. Just as I decided to start hollering for Mama,

Jimmy Wilson came into his backyard. I could see him through the grimy window. He held a kitchen rug way out in front of him, turned his head, closed his eyes and began to shake it for all it was worth.

A lady would have left him alone just then. He was doing a chore for his mother, and he didn't need any interference from me. But I wasn't being a lady. I was on a mission of mercy and needed help. So I cleared my throat and let out a rebel yell, like Tarzan calling Cheetah.

Poor Jimmy dropped that rug and made a beeline for the fence. I swear his face turned white as Bluebeard's ghost even though it was covered with rug dust. He perched up on those pickets for a full minute looking all around like a cat treed by a hound.

I was afraid he'd make a dash for the house, so I hollered out again. "Jimmy Wilson," I screamed as loud as I could, "come over here and help me!"

Only an idiot wouldn't have known it was me, and Jimmy was smarter than that. He glanced at the back door to see if his mother was coming, then jumped into our yard and hurried to the garage.

"What are you yelling for?" he shouted into the empty space where the Nash stayed at night. I guess he didn't see me in the rafters because when I answered him—politely too—he jumped again and landed right smack in the box of curtains.

"I thought it was the voice of God," he told me later. But he couldn't have thought it long because I was right about the spiders. When he jumped into the box, a half dozen of them jumped out. Jimmy hollered and started smashing them as fast as he could. He had on his brother Joe's old hunting boots, so he got all but one before I could explain that we shouldn't kill the spiders because I was on a mission of mercy and people on a mission of mercy couldn't kill anything, and he was my helper so that meant he couldn't kill anything either.

We finally got it all sorted out. Jimmy helped me get the box into the house even though he wasn't supposed to play with me anymore. But we weren't playing, so I guess that was all right. There were spiders in the ornament box too. Mama smashed one and told me not to let another get away, so I guessed my mission of mercy was over and I would have to go back to being a lady.

* * *

I made the costume myself. First I washed the curtains in cool water in the washtub on the mud porch. Papa didn't need the tub anymore since the quarantine sign was gone and he had dinner at the table with the rest of us. Even Chuckie was out of bed and eating like he hadn't ate in weeks, which of course he hadn't. Not much anyway.

When the curtain was dry (I only needed one), it still looked a little yellow, but that didn't matter. It was sort of oblong shaped, bordered on the sides with wide blue piping, with a casing on top and a hem on the bottom. I cut off the piping, folded the curtain in half and cut a half hole where my neck could go. Then I folded the piping in half lengthwise and tied it around my middle like a sash.

Papa said I looked like an angel in that costume. I said I wasn't supposed to be an angel, I was Jesus' mother, Mary. He just winked and said that was okay by him, I was still *his* little angel.

But Papa never made it to the play.

Chapter
Four

What I remember most about that day is walking six blocks from the streetcar to the house in my curtain costume and only one shoe. That, and Papa not coming home at all. He didn't come home for three whole days and when he did he'd forgotten all about the play. It didn't matter anymore anyway on account of everything else going so wrong.

It was all Jeremy Mason's fault. Or anyway, his contrary old mule, Isabel's.

Jeremy played the part of Mary's espoused husband, Joseph. We were supposed to ride into Bethlehem, me on Isabel's back, Jeremy leading her by a short rope. Only Isabel didn't want to go to Bethlehem, she wanted to stay in the gym where she had a bed of hay and a bowl of oats.

I had boy's britches on underneath my costume. Partly because Mama said you could see through the curtain in the light and partly so I wouldn't freeze to death. It was twenty degrees outside and fixing to snow.

Anyway, Isabel refused to leave her bowl of oats. Even when Mrs. Greenwood yanked the bowl away and started walking backward toward the door, Isabel wouldn't budge.

Mrs. Greenwood had to take off to help Stevie Wheeler, one

of the shepherds, find his staff, so Jeremy ran out to the playground and picked a good long switch off the willow tree. He handed me the halter rope.

"My dad says there's only one way to tame a stubborn mule," he said like he knew what he was doing. "When I say go, you pull hard as you can and I'll swat her with the switch."

Well, Jeremy yelled go, and I dug my bare feet into the floor and pulled with all my might. He smacked Isabel across the rump three or four times with that willow switch but all it did was make her mad. She let out a squeal that would have resurrected Grandma Eva and sat right down on the floor. The problem was, Jeremy forgot to get out of the way, and she sat on his foot.

So there we were with Isabel squalling to wake the dead and Jeremy yelling curse words and crying how that cussed mule broke his ankle.

Mrs. Greenwood's face turned red as a Sunday apple. She clamped one hand over Jeremy's mouth and hollered at Stevie Wheeler to go get Mr. Bronx, the janitor.

Thinking to help—though Mama said I wasn't thinking at all or I wouldn't have done it—I grabbed the halo off Sally Jane Reynold's costume. It was just a coat hanger covered in gold pipe cleaners. I straightened it out and gave Isabel one hard jab in the hind end.

She moved all right. Both ends met the middle as she jumped and kicked, knocked me on my fanny, and tried to bite my leg. Tore the seat right out of my britches. In the meantime, Mrs. Greenwood pulled Jeremy free.

Later Mr. Bronx put iodine on Isabel's rump and declared me and Jeremy okay except for bruised dignity, which we were too young to care about anyway and what did we mean by treating a poor defenseless mule like that?

Jeremy and I walked to Bethlehem. Me with torn britches

under my costume and him limping like he'd really walked all the way from Nazareth. Mrs. Greenwood had cookies and cocoa for us afterward and Mama was waiting for me in the gym. Krista already had a cocoa mustache and Chuckie was petting that cussed mule Isabel. I explained to Mama that I had to wear my curtain home on account of my ripped britches.

"That's okay," she said and looked at the watch Papa had given her for their wedding, "but we have to take the streetcar because Papa didn't come home with the car. So hurry now, eat your cookie and find your shoes. We have to go." I could tell she was worried about Papa. She felt sick too. But not as sick as I felt when I went to get my shoes. That stupid Isabel had eaten right through the heel of the left one. It was so chewed up and mangled I could never wear it again.

Mama looked like she was going to cry. So I grabbed Chuckie away from Isabel before she could bite him too, and we walked all the way to the streetcar, then six blocks from the streetcar to home. In twenty degrees and blowing snow, and me with torn britches and only one shoe.

"You'll catch your death, Cissy Marie!" Mama fussed all the way home and went straight for the hot-water bottle to warm my feet.

* * *

It was Krista who got sick. She coughed all that night and all the next day. Mama made a nest of pillows for Chuckie in Krista's bed and put Krista in the crib. Then she made a tent over the crib with an old baby blanket, plopped half a jar of Vicks in the steam water and set it up by Krista's head. It stunk something awful.

Krista cried at first and tore the blanket down, but Mama hushed her and put it back. "You have to keep the blanket there, sweetheart, so the steam can help you breath." She promised Krista a licorice when she got well. Krista liked licorice more than any other candy, so she left the blanket alone. She even took the cough medicine—the kind that tastes like turpentine and burns your throat all the way down—without a whimper.

Mama sat in the rocker beside the crib and cried and prayed. "Lord, please bring Charles home. You know our Krista needs a doctor." Then she looked at Chuckie asleep in Krista's bed and me standing in my nightgown shivering like I was still outside. She closed her eyes again and set the rocker moving hard. "Lord," she prayed out loud, "please keep Chuckie and Cissy well, and bring that man back home where he belongs."

Papa came home the day before Christmas. Only I had to go fetch the doctor 'cause Papa needed one as bad as Krista.

* * *

Dr. Fix was fat. He was fat enough to be the Salvation Army Santa without using any pillows, and that's where I found him on Monday afternoon. He was in front of Mr. Cronkin's hardware store, ringing his bell, collecting money for the Salvation Army, his bald head covered with a red wool hat, his black mustache stiff as an icicle above his fake white beard.

I had to wait until a little kid made his Christmas wish and dropped a penny in the red and white coffee can and Dr. Fix, I mean Santa, handed him a penny candy from the box by the door, said "HO HO HO, Merry Christmas," and sat back down on the sidewalk bench next to the door.

Dr. Fix came right away when I told him Krista was coughing something awful and Papa looked like he'd been in a dog fight and lost.

"Here, Ted," he said, and handed his red wool hat to Mr. Cronkin. "I got to make a house call. You take over for a while."

Poor Mr. Cronkin. I'm not sure what he did, but it would have taken every pillow in Pike to make *him* look like Santa. Papa always said you could pull Ted Cronkin through a straw backwards and he wouldn't get stuck.

Dr. Fix said Krista had the croup. Papa had a broken knuckle and a black eye and a cut on his forehead. Dr. Fix had to take a stitch, and boy did Papa holler!

"Go do that to old man Wilson!" he shouted and tried to knock the doctor's hand away.

"Charles!" Mama looked like she wanted to smack him herself.

Papa ignored her. "That bum's got no call talkin' 'bout my wife like that, or calling me a bloody thief—deserved every bit of what I gave him!"

Mama looked like she was going to faint. She caught sight of me standing in the kitchen doorway. "Cissy," she said all stiff and polite, "go see to the children."

Her eyes said move-right-now, so I did.

Dr. Fix left Papa sleeping and went next door to see about Mr. Wilson. When he came back to fetch his hat, I snuck to the door and heard him say, "Old Man Wilson has a broken jaw." But it turned out neither he nor Papa felt a thing. Dr. Fix said they were both dead drunk and wouldn't know the time of day for a week. By that time Christmas was over, Krista was better, Papa was sleeping on the couch, and I was climbing rafters again to put the Christmas ornaments away.

Thank goodness it was too cold for spiders.

Chapter Five

Our baby was born in March and died in April. Mama stayed in bed for a long long time, and Papa said we had to move in June and she would have to get up and take care of the kids they had left. Meaning me and Krista and Chuckie, of course. Papa didn't mean to be mean. He'd been extra nice to all of us after that Christmas. But he had lost his job at the paper.

Mr. Evans, the owner of the *Pike Review,* had said, "Sorry, but times are tough. Subscriptions are down and I'll have to do the books myself till things look up a bit."

Papa told us, "He studied the holes in the toes of his shoes like he hadn't just put them on this morning, and brightened right up. 'And that'll be soon, you know,' he told us all. 'Why, with Mr. Roosevelt in the White House things are bound to get better fast.' "

We still had to move.

Mama cried. She didn't want to leave our new baby, buried out on Harris Hill, all alone with no one to bring flowers.

"You always said that flowers are for the living," I reminded her. "And baby is with Jesus and Grandma Eva. How can she be lonely?"

Well, Mama couldn't argue, but she still looked sad. She cried some more when we had to leave most of the furniture behind. Even Chuckie's crib and the radio. There was no one with money to buy it, and we could only take what we could carry in the Nash.

* * *

June came faster than streak lightning. By then everything was packed. I fell asleep on a pile of hay spread across the hardwood floor. Mama had complained about the hay. She had scrubbed the house from top to bottom, even washed the windows and cleaned out the wood stove. "A matter of principle," she said. "No one can say I left a dirty house!"

Papa had insisted everything be packed and ready. "We're leaving Sunday afternoon, one o'clock sharp. The sheriff will be here for the keys by then."

That's why I was so surprised when Mama woke me up at eight and handed me my Sunday-school dress. "Put this on." She made me sit up and took away the sheet so I wouldn't go back to sleep. "We may have lost everything we own, but we still have each other and we still have God. I'm thankful for that, and we're going to church this morning to tell him so."

If I was surprised by Mama's announcement, I was flabbergasted to see Papa sitting in the kitchen, wearing his Sunday suit and eating one of Mrs. Wilson's farewell huckleberry muffins.

We hadn't been to church in weeks. Not since the baby died. And Papa hadn't been since Christmas. He'd taken to staying out late on Saturday nights. On Sunday mornings he was always feeling poorly and slept till we got home at noon. Prohibition had been over for a while, and Mama said we'd rue the day they made liquor legal again.

But this morning Papa seemed like his old self. He ruffled Krista's hair and called her Pumpkin. He broke off chunks of muffin and fed them to Chuckie, and said I looked like an angel in my white cotton dress with the bright pink sash.

Mama wore the black rayon she'd bought for Grandma Eva's funeral. She piled her shiny brown hair up on her head so the white didn't show at all, and even put on lipstick and face powder. Papa said she looked like she was going to a party. Mama blushed pink under the powder and shooed us out to the car.

We all had to ride in front. That old Nash was piled so high you couldn't fit a penny between my mattress and the roof. I sat between Mama and Papa and held Chuckie on my lap. Krista sat on Mama's knees and held onto the dash. She left her hand prints on the glove box in the dust, and once we stepped inside the church Mama had to take her straight to the bath-room to wash.

Sunday school was crowded. I took Chuckie to the nursery and by the time I got to class there was only one seat left—right in the middle of the front row. I turned around to hustle out the door. I could help hold babies in the nursery, and anyway I'd already said good-by to all my friends.

But Miss Goodwin saw me.

"Cissy Summers!" she crowed, right in front of all those kids. "I'm so glad you came today; we've missed you."

Everyone stopped talking and watched as she took me by the shoulders and led me to the seat up front.

Susi Cummings giggled and nudged Judy Thomas with her elbow, and I gave them both a look that would freeze fire. They shut up after that and folded their hands in their laps like ladies, which I knew they weren't because they were both in my class at school and went out of their way to torment Mary Beth Watkins, who is fat and ugly and has a hair growing right out of a mole on her cheek, and who was sitting in the seat right next to the one Miss Goodwin plunked me down in.

They didn't laugh, though. And after class Susi even gave me her brother's old Boy Scout badge "to remember me by," she said and wiped away a real tear.

The lesson was on Hebrews 13:5 where God said, "I will never leave thee, nor forsake thee."

"Never forget that, Cissy." Miss Goodwin took me aside after class. "Never forget that God loves you. No matter what happens, he will never leave you!"

And I never did forget, not exactly. But I wondered for a while if he was really there, and if he was, why he didn't stop some things from happening. I still wonder that.

Chapter
Six

We piled back in the Nash right after Sunday school, and left our home in Pike, Nevada, forever.

Papa started whistling as soon as we crossed the border into California. We had to stop for gas in Barstow because the Nasty Nash guzzled gasoline like it didn't cost eighteen cents a gallon. When we pulled up to the pumps, Papa handed Mama a dollar bill for gas and hurried over to the pay phone nailed on the corner of the hardware store.

It was beastly hot. A long-eared hound lay panting underneath the plank-board porch. The way his tongue hung down, all wet and dripping on the dirt, gave me a powerful thirst. A sign in the window flashed *Coca Cola* in big, round, cursive letters. *Coca Cola—5¢ a glass.* I begged Mama for a nickel. "I'll share with Chuckie and Krista," I promised.

Mama glanced at Papa through the open window, then dug into her handbag and handed me a coin. Not a nickel, though; a shiny dime! Enough to buy two Cokes to share.

I hopped and skipped across the blacktop. The sun-hot gravel stung my toes and I was in a hurry to reach that wooden porch.

Papa didn't see me; his back was to the door. I would have scooted right on by, but a big blond kid came barreling through the rusty screen door. Nearly knocked me flat. Mama's dime rolled through a knothole and I had to crawl under there to find it.

I couldn't help but hear Papa's voice. He was talking loud enough to wake the hound.

"What do you mean, that's my share?" His voice got low and growly. "You owe me another grand. I'll be there Monday morning. You'd better have it all!"

I had no idea what a grand was. Right then, that big old hound took to licking me on the face. I yucked and yicked and spit in the dirt. The next thing I knew, Papa had me by the arm and yanked me out onto the pavement.

"Don't ever listen to my phone calls again," he yelled, slapping me hard across the cheek.

I couldn't believe my precious Papa hit me! I stood there with my chin down to my knees and watched Papa stomp off to the car. "What did I do?" I wondered and rubbed my cheek up by my ear where it burned the most.

Mama motioned me to come. I hip-hopped back across the fire-hot pavement, then remembered the dime. When I turned around, the big blond kid stood grinning ear to ear, flipping something shiny-silver high into the air. My dime. He caught it in his cap, brought his hand up in a one-finger salute, and marched into the store.

The hound dog scratched an ear and crawled back underneath the porch.

* * *

We left the store and drove till it was night. Papa stopped to buy a copy of the *Examiner*. He never did say he was sorry for hitting me, but he bought us each a hot dog and smiled when he handed me a Coke.

We propped ourselves against the plaster wall and licked the mustard from our fingers. I ate my hot dog slow. First a bite of bun and then a tiny bite of meat. If you didn't push the wiener up each time you took a bite, it slid into the paper until all you had was soggy bun. I was showing Krista how to do it when Chuckie started to cry. He'd done it wrong and dropped his wiener in the dirt. I knew he wouldn't get another so I picked it up and hurried to the water hose. I rinsed off all the dirt, but it washed away the mustard too and Chuckie didn't want it back.

Papa came to see what all the howling was about. "Come on, babycakes," he said and swung Chuckie to his shoulder. "I'll give you a horsey ride. Here, Cissy, take this to the car for me." He handed me the paper.

Chuckie squealed while Papa neighed and pranced around the yard. Krista jumped up and down in the dirt. "Me too, Papa. Me next!" Mama shook her head at them and laughed the way she used to laugh before Papa lost his job and the baby died. All light and happy, like the tinkling of the front doorbell.

I thought how the day had turned out good after all. That is, until I read some of the *Examiner*.

The picture on the front of the paper almost made me throw away my hot dog. "Captain Frank Hamer Captures Bonnie and Clyde," the headline said. They didn't look captured to me; they looked dead. Blood all over the place. And that old car so full of bullet holes it wouldn't hold water. It looked like Mrs. Wilson's washtub after Mr. Wilson cornered a possum and took after it with the scatter gun. Only there wasn't any blood 'cause the possum got away. Mr. Wilson was mad about that, and he had to buy Mrs. Wilson a new washtub to boot.

Mama saw the picture and took the paper away. "The children shouldn't see this, Charles," she said and handed it back to Papa. Papa nodded. He stuffed it underneath the driver's seat and started up the Nash. Chuckie fell right off to sleep and Krista pouted 'cause she never got her turn at horsey.

I sat there in the darkness, staring out the grimy window, and watched the stars pop out all over the sky, and thought how sad it must be to die. I asked God, "Are Bonnie and Clyde in heaven?"

Somehow I didn't think so and it made me want to cry.

* * *

"We can't stay here, Charles," Mama whispered when she saw the camp we pulled into that night. I agreed and looked at Papa. When I saw his face, I knew we were doomed. Now I really wanted to cry. Mama did cry. The ground was soggy and stunk like an outhouse on a summer afternoon. The little patch of grass was yellow-brown and stung my feet worse than the gravel had in Barstow.

Papa dragged the mattress from the car and plopped it on the grass. Then he made a tent with sticks and blankets.

"There," he said. "You and Krista crawl in, Cissy. You'll sleep fine in there till morning."

Some boys ran by, kicking up the stinky dirt, pointing willow sticks and yelling, "Bang bang, you're dead!"

"I'm a G-man," one screamed and shook his stick at me. "I'm going to blow your head off!"

I was about to show him how it'd feel to lose a head when his mama came and grabbed him by the ear. He set up a yowl as she dragged him back across the road. I laughed and felt better until I saw my own mama's face. I grabbed Krista by the hand and dove into our makeshift tent.

When I woke up the next morning, Mama and Chuckie were asleep on the other side of Krista. Samantha's foot had got tangled in my hair, and I was almost off the mattress. Papa and the Nash were gone.

I found a note pinned to the pillowcase that held my things: underwear, socks and my almost-new pink cotton dress. I guess Papa didn't look inside or he'd have known it was mine, not

Mama's. I pretended not to see "Lynetta" printed on the front; after all, the note was on *my* bag. "I'll be back for you soon," was all it said—or all I had time to read anyway. I felt Mama's hand on my shoulder and folded it up quick. I thought I was in trouble sure, but she just read the note and closed her eyes. When she opened them again they glinted hard like steel flints.

Actually I read that in a book. Mama's eyes were blue. Bluer than mine. "They could cut you to the soul," my Grandma Eva always said. Grandma Eva was her mother, and I guess she would know. They just looked unusually hard right then—Mama's eyes, I mean. Then she rolled the note up in a ball and tucked it in the pocket of her travel skirt.

"Get the little ones," she said and grabbed our pillowcases one by one. She handed each of us a towel and me the soap. Ivory soap, a clean new bar. Krista ran back to get Samantha and we followed Mama to the creek that ran behind the camp. Even poor Samantha got a scrubbing. Krista howled when Mama took the doll away, but it had fallen in the dirt and might have picked up germs.

We used the facilities. I'd have rather dug a hole down by the creek, but Mama said that wasn't civilized. Then we scrubbed our hands and feet, and washed our hair. I bit my lip until it bled when Mama combed it out. She braided it in back, then piled the braid up on my head. "It will stay cleaner that way," she said, and did the same to Krista.

Chuckie had two baths before it all was done. He got away while Mama was braiding my hair and fell down in the dirt. Krista had to leave Samantha drying on a tree stump while she took her nap. Mama set me to some lessons in an old *McGuffey Reader* and went across the way to talk to the pretend G-man's mother.

What a miserable two days! That was how long it took before Papa came back, all smiles and dressed to the nines. Even the

Nash was clean. "Fellow at the station hosed it off because I got a fill-up," Papa said. "Washed the windows too!"

Chuckie ran to hug his legs and Krista showed him Samantha's clean clothes.

I pouted some because I'd have rather been with Papa in town than sleeping in a blanket tent and scrubbing in the creek. But I stopped pouting when Papa handed me an apple and a real sandwich. One with butter and bologna and lettuce and cheese. And licorice taffy for dessert!

Mama had gone quiet again. She took her sandwich and looked at Papa, her head cocked to one side, her eyes asking questions I couldn't even guess.

"I got a job," he said, and looked away from Mama's eyes.

He swung Chuckie high into the air. Chuckie squealed and spit up grape juice on his shirt, but Papa didn't seem to care. "I got a job," he said again. "With a meat packing company in Los Angeles. They needed a bookkeeper; hired me on the spot. A thousand a year and a house to boot."

"They gave you money up-front, Charles?" Mama asked.

"An advance, Lynetta, and more to come." He looked at her, his eyes all squinty sad.

Mama sighed and laid her head against his shoulder. Krista closed her eyes, chewed her licorice slow, and licked the drippings from her chin.

Chapter
Seven

Our new house on York Street in Highland Park was so much like the one in Pike, I had to blink twice when I saw it. It had the same wide cement porch, right down to the dirty gray paint peeling off the steps. Only the house in Nevada had two steps and this one in California had three on account of it sitting at the top of a hill. Well, not a hill exactly, more like a slope. But enough of a slope for Chuckie to trip and roll all the way back to the sidewalk. Mama's face turned gray as the porch, but Chuckie just pushed up to his knees, laughing and screeching, and started to crawl back up to do it all over again.

I thought it looked like fun, but one look at Mama's face and I knew I hadn't better try it just then. Krista sat down prim and proper on the grass and introduced Samantha to some crickets in the ivy. She was too much of a little lady to roll down hills. Even at the age of six.

Papa scooped up Chuckie and propped him on his shoulders. They galloped up the front porch steps, Papa snorting and whinnying. He was supposed to be a horse, only he sounded more like Jeremy's old mule, Isabel.

Inside, the house was bigger than the one in Pike. It was dark and had a dusty smell, like the windows had been nailed shut for months. Mama went from room to room pushing back the soot-smudged curtains and pulling up the shades. She clucked her tongue and shook her head at the dust balls on the hardwood floors.

"They must have had a dog in here, Charles," she said, looking at the living-room rug. "There's a puppy stain on the carpet." I didn't know how she saw it. That rug looked like a flower garden. Dark red and blue and green roses all swirled together so you had to look close to see what the pattern was. I bent down to look and backed up quick. You didn't have to see the puppy stain; it smelled like a run-over skunk.

But the curtains and shades were nice. We never had those in Nevada. And the kitchen! So big and bright even Mama had to smile. "Look, Charles," she said, "so many cupboards and such a pretty yellow. Why, I'll never be able to fill them up. And a brand new ice box. Not a speck of rust."

We turned back into the dining room and Mama stopped so fast I had to say "sorry" for bumping into her back. I ducked under her arm to see what she was gaping at and my own chin fell right down to my chest.

It was the most beautiful cabinet I'd ever seen, built right in the wall. Two sets of double glass doors, all carved with milk-white flowers, stems and leaves and all. And little white china knobs for handles.

Mama sucked in air. "Oh, Charles," she breathed, "a real china cupboard!" She buried her face in Papa's shoulder and started to cry.

Krista hugged Samantha tight and rocked her hard. Chuckie started to whimper, and Papa rolled his eyes up to the ceiling. "Now, Lynetta," he scolded, patting her back a couple of times, "don't take on. You're frightening the children."

Mama tried to smile and searched her bosom for a hanky. Papa handed her his and set Chuckie on the floor. I looked at the china cabinet and the empty old-new house, and understood how Mama felt. We had to leave our baby and our home in Pike, but it looked like things might be much nicer here in California.

* * *

We'd only been there two days and I wanted to run away. At least as far as the park. It was only two blocks down and some boys with the WPA were mowing the grass and putting up monkey bars and mending the swings.

I had to ask Papa what WPA was and he said, "It's the president's new program for people without jobs." I thought it was nice of Mr. Roosevelt to give those people jobs and said so. But Papa just hurumphed and went back to his paper.

I told Mama, "How about if I get the little ones out of your hair and go see if the swings are ready?" But she just smiled and handed me another rag. "Not until we're done," she said.

I thought it would take forever. We scrubbed and rubbed and polished that old house—nearly took the paint right off the walls. No spider could live in our window sills. Mama even got the "puppy stain" out of the rug. The red and blue and green flowers faded to a rusty blob as big as the ham platter, but Mama said she would rather have that spot than have the whole house smell like a dead skunk, and anyway, we could cover it with a scatter rug.

I had just rubbed the last glob of wax into the hardwood floor in me and Krista's room, when I heard a commotion out front. I tiptoed down the hall. Mama had just waxed it too, and I didn't want to land bottom over tea kettle against the bathroom door. I'd already done that once and it wasn't any fun.

I peeked out the living-room window. Mama stood on the porch arguing with a huge hairy man in blue overalls and no shirt. My heart started pounding and I thought how we didn't have a telephone and I couldn't call the police and what would I do if that man hurt Mama?

But Mama didn't look scared, just confused, waving her arms and shaking her head and pointing at the dust-covered white truck parked at the bottom of our hill. The man kept nodding yes and wiped the sweat off his face onto his dirty overalls.

At this house, the Nash lived in a falling-down shack at the bottom of the slope, and I thought Mama might be upset because that big old truck was blocking the driveway and Papa was due home any minute.

Then I saw two younger men. One crawled in the back of the truck and handed something down. I squinted into the sun, then let out a whoop. "Bed springs," I hollered loud enough for Jimmy Wilson to hear, and him back in Pike. "A real bed!"

I let the curtain drop and bolted for the door. I was down that hill so fast I would have rolled if I hadn't been flying.

"Cissy!" I heard Mama call but I couldn't stop, so I pretended not to hear and climbed up in the truck. It looked like Mr. Cronkin's hardware store and a furniture store to boot. Four beds, a sofa and a chest of drawers. A tall, brass floor lamp with a pleated shade, and a painted yellow table with four straight-back chairs.

When I hopped out of the truck, dancing a jig and acting five instead of almost twelve, Papa pulled up behind the truck and saved both the hairy man and me a licking.

Chapter
Eight

With all the furniture in place and the old-new house scrubbed "clean enough to please the president," as Papa said, Mama said it finally seemed like home. "But Mr. Roosevelt's not invited," she teased. "Him and his smelly old cigars!"

Krista changed Samantha's clothes on the new sofa and I plugged in the lamp. We put it on the faded spot, and the puppy stain didn't show a bit. Chuckie toddled over to the table and started pounding on a brown cardboard box someone had left sitting on a chair.

"No!" Papa hollered, and we all froze. Chuckie's face screwed up in a pitiful pout and Papa hurried over to pick him up. "Come see, Lynetta." Papa patted Chuckie and looked at Mama, eyes dancing like a firefly on a starry night.

I cried. I couldn't help it, 'cause if Papa had given her the moon, he couldn't have pleased Mama more. The box was full of dishes: plates in two sizes, cups and saucers and little round glazed bowls for fruit. They were porcelain china, the color of new-drawn cream, with raised pink roses. The petals looked real enough to smell.

Mama placed a setting in the glass-door cabinet, then stood back to admire it from every angle. Papa dug deep into the box and pulled out salt and pepper shakers and a butter dish to match. He looked at her like a puppy waiting to be praised, and my heart swelled up inside my chest. I was proud of Papa then. So proud and glad I could almost bust.

* * *

We finally made it to the park. Almost every day from July to the end of August. It never rained. Not once. The grass got brown and stubby dry but the playground was almost finished. There was gravel beneath the merry-go-round and the swings, and sawdust by the slide and monkey bars.

My birthday was a week away, and school too. I felt nervous and excited all at once and really didn't want to go to the park that day. I would have rather stayed home to climb the apple tree and eat green fruit and read a book. It would take my mind off going to a new school and having new teachers and meeting new friends.

But Chuckie whined and Krista hung her head. Mama felt sick again and went back to bed after breakfast, so we went to the park.

Some husky boys in dirty undershirts and dungarees were digging out a sandbox and framing it with wooden slats. I pushed Chuckie on the swings and watched awhile until they took a break. Krista was playing on the merry-go-round over by the benches, when a red-haired kid in baggy shorts pushed the thing too fast. Krista squealed and bounced off right onto the gravel.

I left Chuckie in the baby swing and ran to help Krista up, only one of the workers got there first and was already wiping her skinned knee with an oily gray handkerchief. I was torn between belting that bratty red-haired kid and comforting Krista when the worker looked up. "She's all right, just a little scrape," he said.

When he saw me, his mouth snapped shut and his eyes got

—47—

all squinty mean. He just sat there on his haunches, with his bloody handkerchief pressed against Krista's knee, and glared. You'd have thought I was a garden snake that just swallowed his pet mouse.

I backed off and stammered, "She's my little sister." Then I knew where I'd seen him before.

"You're Susi Cummings's big brother," I blurted out. "We lived three blocks from you in Pike, Nevada." I pulled Krista up against my legs.

"I know who you are." His voice got low and growly. "And I have a message for your father."

He looked like a giant when he stood. A sunburnt giant with greasy black hair and a nasty scar across his cheek. Big enough to break my neck if he'd wanted to. What I wanted was to run, but I'd have had to drag Krista, who was still sobbing and brushing gravel off her knees, and collect Chuckie from the baby swing. So I just stood still and wondered why Roy Cummings was so mad at me.

"You tell your father," he growled, shaking his finger in my face, "that he's gonna pay for what he did to me. I've got connections, and I'll see that he pays. You tell him, Sis. You hear?"

I swallowed the lump in my throat and nodded like I knew what he meant and watched that finger. It was black and caked with dirt under the nail. Susi's mother would have whopped him good if he'd come home like that.

That thought made me feel braver. I grabbed Krista's hand and pulled her to her feet. "I'm not your sis!" I hollered over my shoulder as I led her away. The other workers stared but I didn't care. I lifted Chuckie from the baby swing, cool as you please, and strolled out of the park like I hadn't just had the worst scare of my whole entire life!

My heart was pounding. Thumping like a drum at a Fourth of July parade. "What did he mean?" I prayed to God. "Why is Susi Cummings's brother mad at Papa?"

* * *

I didn't want to tell Papa. I thought how Roy Cummings must have made a mistake and thought I was someone else. Someone else's father was in trouble. But I knew it wasn't true. I remembered Mrs. Wilson telling everyone in town it was Papa's fault the bank crashed, and how Jimmy Wilson couldn't play with me for weeks.

I tossed and turned for two whole nights and didn't sleep a wink. I wasn't going to say a word, but Mama said I looked "peaked" and probably just needed cleaning out, and headed for the castor oil. I had to tell her.

Mama's face got white and quiet. She hurried to the bathroom, shut the door and turned the water on full blast.

Papa had already left for work. I knew Mama was sick again and thought how I'd better keep the little ones quiet and out of her hair.

Chuckie finished his oatmeal and crawled down from the table. I handed him the sailboat I'd made from a sardine can for his three-year-old birthday. It had a sucker-stick mast and a paper sail. Chuckie ran straight to the service porch and dropped it in the washtub full of water.

Krista begged for a bandage to put on Samantha's knee. "Samantha fell off the merry-go-round too, Cissy," she said. "She should have a bandage just like mine." So I found a soft, white hankie in the rag bag and tore off a strip to tie around her dolly's leg.

Mama finally came out of the bathroom, her eyes all red and puffy. The smile she'd worn all summer was gone again. She looked tired and sad. She put her arm around my shoulders and gave a gentle squeeze. "Don't worry, Cissy. Everything will be all right. I'll talk to your father." She put her fingers under my chin and looked deep into my eyes. "If you see Roy again, just walk away. Fast as you can, you hear?" I nodded yes.

"And don't let him in the house." She jiggled my chin to make sure I was paying attention. I didn't take my eyes off her face. "Don't ever let anyone in the house, especially a stranger. Understand?"

I gulped and nodded yes again. Mama kissed me on my hair and said I was a good girl and would I please watch the little ones. She had to go lay down awhile.

I knew then that something else was really wrong. Papa was in bad trouble. Worse than when he came home dead drunk last Christmas.

The happy summer in our old-new house was over.

Chapter
Nine

After Mama talked to Papa, he took to drinking whiskey almost every day. I wondered how a person could stand to feel dizzy and sick all the time. Once was enough for me. Jake Freeman had found one of Papa's bottles and we shared it. It was fun at first, but afterwards I felt like I'd been run over by the Nash.

Jake lived next door to me on York Street. There are eight or nine Freeman kids, I never could keep count, and Jake's the oldest and the nicest of the lot. I liked him right away even if his ears are too big for his face and his nose looks like he ran into a brick wall.

I asked Jake if that's what happened 'cause Judy Thomas's brother did—run into a brick wall, I mean. He went skiing for the first time ever on Humble Mountain. Judy said he did a real good job of staying up all the way down the hill, but he forgot to learn how to stop and ran smack into the side of the brick lodge. Flattened his nose all over his face. Left some skin on the wall too, Judy said.

Jake laughed when I asked did he run into a wall too. "No," he said, "I broke it in a fight," and kind of tucked his thumbs under his belt and stuck his chin way out like he was proud.

"You should have seen the other guy," he grinned. "He don't have no front teeth to this very day!"

Jake knew a lot about life 'cause he spent most of his time in town or on the sand lot on the corner trying to keep out of his mother's way. With seven or eight brothers and sisters there was always a chore she wanted him to do.

One day I found him hiding in the shack where Papa parks the Nash. Sitting in the corner, big as you please, tipping a bottle to his lips. He started to run till he saw it was me. Then he just grinned and said, "Come on in, we'll have some fun."

"Jake Freeman," I sputtered like a frightened goose, "what are you doing in here?"

He ran his fingers through his mussed-up hair and cleared his throat twice before he answered. "Uh . . . I was looking for my brother Timmy." He wiped his mouth with his shirttail and smiled. "Yah. I was just out looking for Tim-boy and I thought I saw him duck in here."

Jake peered around the inside of the shack like he expected Tim to pop out any minute. "Guess he didn't, though," he said and held out the square, brown bottle in his hand. "While I was searching for Tim, I found this stashed behind that pile of bricks." He slouched back against the wall and patted the dirt beside him. "Come and keep me company. Ma'll have my hide 'cause I never found Tim, so I thought I'd just hole up in here awhile until she forgets about both of us."

"I'm sort of hiding too," I told Jake. "Mama has to take Krista on the streetcar to the shoe store and I know if I'm around she'll ask me to watch Chuckie, and I don't want to right now." Mama had said that morning how I was being contrary lately, and what was wrong with me, and where was her sweet little girl always ready to help?

"I don't know what's wrong with me," I said to Jake, and sat beside him on the ground. "I just sometimes want to be alone.

Sometimes I feel mad and sometimes I want to cry for no good reason."

Jake nodded and patted my knee. "I know what you mean, Cissy," he said. "I can't ever find a place to be alone either. Ma says I should be thankful to have such a nice big family, but all those kids . . ." He shook his head and took another drink from the bottle.

"It's like a circus, you know? Always someone to feed or doctor or chase down for a bath. And Pa says I'm responsible to help 'cause I'm the oldest. Ma's always on my back about schoolwork, but how'm I supposed to get any work done with all the chores, let alone the noise?"

His voice got louder and louder and I had to interrupt and tell him, "Shush, or you'll have your mama *and* mine in here!" It was the longest speech I'd ever heard from Jake. I guess he realized it too, 'cause he closed his eyes and stayed quiet for a while.

I thought he'd gone to sleep, and I was about to creep out of the shack to see if Mama had gone, when Jake sat up straight and thrust the bottle into my hands.

"Here, have some," he said, grinning. "It'll make you feel good."

The whiskey tasted terrible. Like turpentine or Dr. Fix's cough medicine. Burned something awful all the way down! I coughed and sputtered like a dying cat, but I took another swallow to be friendly, and pretty soon Jake and I were laughing and singing and swatting each other on the arm.

"The one who feels a sting has to take another swallow from the bottle," Jake said and took another swig. But after three or four, I couldn't feel anything and had to close my eyes to keep the rafters still. They kept wanting to tumble down the walls into the dirt and crawl back up again, swinging and swaying like the wood slats on a rollercoaster track.

When I woke up, Jake was gone and I heard Mama calling from the porch. It was almost dark outside, but I couldn't get up. Every time I moved I thought I'd died and gone to hell. "Would serve me right," I told myself.

Then I thought I heard the Nash coming up the road. What would Papa do if he found me? I knew it wouldn't be anything nice, so I crawled across the dirt, out of the shack and into the hedge that separated our house from the one next door. Jake's house, the snake. I took to blaming him for my painful head and rocky stomach.

But it wasn't Papa's car I heard. In fact, he never did come home that night. Mama cried. I don't know if it was for me or Papa. I'd have felt better if she'd hit me or yelled or something, but after I finished throwing up all over the bathroom, she just handed me a rag, said, "Clean up the mess," and cried.

I prayed to Jesus every morning and every night for a week to tell him sorry. "I won't ever do that again, I promise. Never!"

And for a long time I never wanted to.

* * *

Things happened so fast that fall it made my head spin without the whiskey. I turned twelve and Krista started school. She was scared the first day and upchucked her egg all over the sidewalk. I just handed her a napkin from my lunch sack and walked her on. I knew how she felt. My own stomach felt shaky at the thought of a new school.

"I'm proud of you," I said to make her feel better. "You're a big girl now. You'll learn to read and write, and you can show the teacher how you draw!" That made her smile. Krista loved to draw, especially cats and houses and dolls.

I really was proud of her. She hadn't even cried when Mama made her leave Samantha home. She just handed her beloved doll to Chuckie and told him to take care of her "like a good papa." Chuckie nodded and crossed his heart, but I wasn't sure it was the best thing to do. Chuckie wasn't always careful with his toys, and could a three-year-old be a good papa, even to a doll? He did fine for a couple weeks, but then Samantha disappeared. Chuckie didn't know where she went and Krista tried hard not to cry. I decided to make Krista another doll.

I saved my corn cob from supper, cut the pointed end with Mama's kitchen knife to make the legs, and laid it in the sun to dry. Then I sewed on button eyes and cornsilk hair. I even found a ribbon in the rag box, and Jake borrowed one of his grandpa's pipe cleaners for the arms.

I knew this doll could never replace Samantha, but Krista said, "Thank you," and tried to smile, and named the doll Cecilia for a friend at school.

* * *

The real G-men shot a man named Baby Face Nelson and one called Pretty Boy Floyd. We studied it in a class called Current Events. I don't know why they called them "Pretty Boy" and "Baby Face." They were grown men and bad. Miss Lawrence, my seventh-year teacher, said they deserved to die. They were criminals and had done horrible things to people.

Roy Cummings said my Papa did bad things to people. I wondered, "Does Papa deserve to die?" I surely didn't think so, and I spent a lot of time that year feeling sad and scared.

We studied about the Barrow gang too. I told Miss Lawrence I'd read it in the *Examiner*—how they were killed and all—and how it had a picture and a poem, only I didn't get to read it all on account of Mama taking the paper away before I got the chance. Well, Miss Lawerence called Mama to see if we still had the paper and could I bring it to school now that I was older, so we could study it in Current Events?

Mama didn't want to, I could tell. She said as how that was several months ago and would qualify as history better than current events, but she would ask Papa if the paper was still around. Papa gave the paper over and I took it to school. Mama wasn't pleased, but what could she do? Miss Lawrence let me stand up front and read the poem that Bonnie wrote:

Now Bonnie and Clyde are the Barrow gang,
   I'm sure you all have read
How they rob and steal,
And how those who squeal,
Are usually found dying or dead. . . .
If they try to act like citizens
   And rent them a nice little flat,
About the third night they are invited to fight
By a submachine gun rat-tat-tat.
Someday they will go down together,
   And they will bury them side by side.
To a few it means grief,
To the law it's relief,
But it is death to Bonnie and Clyde.

Mary Perkins thought the poem romantic, at least the part about them going down together. Sally Ross had to be excused when she saw the picture. The boys all went around rat-a-tatting at recess and Miss Lawrence said it should be a lesson to anyone who thinks to break the law—"God's or man's," she said.

I thought it was sad. "How does it feel?" I asked God. "How does it feel to know you're going to die?"

Chapter Ten

Papa sometimes gave us each a dime for the Saturday movies: Tom Mix, Flash Gordon or Tarzan. Usually only Krista and I went; Chuckie was too little. But then a cartoon came out called Donald Duck and Mama said how Chuckie could go if we were very careful and held his hand and took him to the bathroom at intermission.

Chuckie sure did love that cartoon. He started with a giggle, but when that funny duck in sailor clothes started to sing, Chuckie laughed. He laughed so hard he wet his britches and made a fuss when I tried to take him out. So I let him be. Krista and I laughed too. And then Tarzan came on and Chuckie still wouldn't let us leave, and I was worried that Mama would be mad 'cause Chuckie had wet britches and I didn't bring him home. But we stayed.

For three whole hours Chuckie hooted and hollered with the rest of us, and we could never leave him home again! Papa had to come up with one more dime on Saturday morning, and Mama threw up her hands and said how we'd created a monster.

"That boy plays Tarzan all day long," Mama complained to Papa. "And he sings like Donald Duck. At three years old! I can't get him to talk in a normal voice."

"He's a boy, Lynetta. Leave him be!" And Papa would hand us each a dime and go back to his paper or leave the house for his "Saturday job," which we all knew was down at Keyhole Nelson's Bar. They called him Keyhole because only certain people could get in the bar. You had to knock on the door and someone would look out at you through a slot in the door that looked like a keyhole to see if you could come in or not.

I know because I did it on a dare one day when Jake and I took the streetcar into town to buy a ball and jacks for his father's birthday. I said I didn't think his father would still play with jacks, but Jake just smiled and said, "It's the thought that counts," and winked at me in a way I knew meant he was up to something.

We had to walk right by Keyhole Nelson's Bar, and Jake said everybody knew my papa went there, and he bet Papa was there now. I said, "He is not," even though I knew he probably was.

"Prove it!" Jake said really loud. I told him, "Hush!" and asked him, "How?"

"Just knock on the door," he said, bold as you please.

I was scared. I didn't want to knock on that door. What if they let me in? What if Papa was there and I saw him? Worse, what if Jake saw him, and all the other passers-by? But Jake whispered, "Dare ya!" so I marched right up and knocked, 'cause I couldn't let Jake see I was scared or he'd think Papa was there for sure. What a pickle!

When I knocked, an eye looked through the keyhole slot and didn't see me, so I knocked again and this time the eye yelled, "Go away!" and I ran. I ran so fast I beat Jake to the streetcar stop and he spent half the way home trying to catch his breath. He never dared me after that.

* * *

It finally cooled off sometime in December. We had blankets on the bed at night and I wore a sweater to school. No snow, though. I thought it was just as well, 'cause I wasn't partial to wearing boy's britches under my school dress!

There was no school play either. We had a choir instead. Three choirs altogether. One for the primary kids, one for the middle grades and one for upperclassmen—that was me.

Krista's group sang "Silent Night" and "Away in a Manger." They looked so sweet, it didn't matter if they sounded like a nest of new-hatched sparrows. Krista knew all the words, and the program went great until one of Jake's little brothers hollered out, "What's a virgin, teacher?" Like he'd never pondered it before or had a chance to ask.

All the parants laughed, except for Jake's mother. His teacher, Mrs. Bowman, ignored him and went right on with the song, but the back of her neck sprouted little red blotches. I could see them from where I was sitting in the front row. I wondered what her face looked like. Of course, I laughed with all the others, like I knew what a virgin was. I thought how I would have to look it up in the dictionary after school started again in January.

Papa came to the concert. He smiled and clapped and even stayed awake—especially when Marie Harris sang "O Holy Night" one key higher than the piano. What's more, he came home every night for two whole weeks.

When Papa promised Chuckie something special for his fourth birthday, on Christmas Eve, Chuckie was impossible for three whole days. Mama finally let him open his present early. Chuckie tore the store-bought paper off the box and dumped his present on the floor. For a minute he just sat and stared. Then he let out a whoop that would make Tarzan jealous.

I pushed in front of Papa so I could see, and all I could say was, "Wow." Mama said, "Oh, Charles, no!" and looked away, her face gone white again.

Chuckie started jumping up and down, trying to get the belt buckled on his new, real leather holster. I knew it was real leather 'cause of the smell. Papa laughed and told him to quit wiggling. Chuckie quit just long enough for Papa to fasten the clasp, then he picked up the shiny silver cap pistol and loaded it like he'd been doing it for years.

He fired the first cap. Mama hollered, "Mercy!" and waved away the smoke. Papa laughed and said, "Not inside, cowboy, take it on the porch."

Meanwhile Krista sat hunched over on the couch and picked cornhairs from Cecilia's chest. I could tell she was still upset about losing Samantha, but she would never say anything to Chuckie.

Chapter
Eleven

I got roller skates for Christmas. Chuckie got a brand-new scooter and Krista got Tarzan. Tarzan was the biggest of Millie's six kittens, and Millie was the Freemans' tiger cat. She had gray and white stripes and soft green eyes. She was gentle and sweet, a real ladycat, except for twice a year when she went a little crazy. She would yowl and rub against anything in sight: the fencepost, Mama's rose bushes, anybody's ankle. Set up a commotion you could hear from here to Tuesday.

That kitty liked our house. Too many whisker-pulling hands and tail-stomping feet at hers. At ours, Krista was always petting her. So Mama let Krista bring her on the service porch for a once-in-a-while saucer of milk, but she wasn't allowed anywhere else in the house. "The best place for a cat is nowhere," Papa always said. So Krista was careful to keep Millie out of sight.

One day Krista left the door open a crack when she went in to warm the milk, and Millie slipped through. Krista said later she thought the kitty had gone back outside. It wasn't until after supper, when we were listening to the Lone Ranger and his faithful companion, Tonto, on the radio, that we found her. Millie, I mean.

The Lone Ranger had just called, "Hi Ho Silver, away!" when Mama said, "Land, Charles, what's that smell?"

Papa sniffed and cocked his head toward the lamp. "What's that noise?" he asked, and snapped off the radio.

"Kitties!" Chuckie squealed and pointed behind the sofa.

"Millie!" Krista screamed. "Mama, Millie's dying!" And she buried her face in Mama's skirt.

"Oh, my stars." Mama said quietly. That was as close to cursing as Mama ever got.

I won't tell what Papa said.

"Charles, hush! The children!" Mama could rise to any situation, Grandma Eva always used to say. "Krista, be quiet. Millie isn't dying at all. Chuckie, settle down or I'll pop your bottom."

Then she turned to me. "Cissy, go get a box and that old bath rug from the rag bag, then go tell your friend Jake to come fetch his cats."

I didn't need to be told twice. Jake took the kitties home and Krista cried for days. She wouldn't eat her supper, and Papa said how this was the most exasperating mess he'd ever seen.

"Do something with that youngster, Lynetta," Papa scowled from behind the evening paper. "Can't a man have peace in his own home?"

"I'm trying, Charles," Mama sighed and sent Krista to our room.

"She wants a kitty, Papa," I said real quiet. "She thinks Millie's hurt and dying."

Papa hated to see any of us cry, couldn't stand it at all. He rolled his eyes, set the paper down and left the table.

Christmas morning, Krista found Tarzan in her stocking. She named him that because not an hour after Christmas breakfast he took to swinging on Mama's clean white sheers.

Papa said the kitty should belong to us anyway seeing as how Millie had him on our living-room carpet. Right behind the sofa and next to the lamp that hid the puppy stain.

Mama got a sewing machine for Christmas. Papa said she could save money by sewing clothes for us. But Mama didn't smile. "How, Charles? Where did you get the money for all these things?" I heard her whisper while they picked up crumpled wrapping paper and shredded bows.

Papa looked tired and cross. "Let it go, Lynetta. It's Christmas. Just let it go."

That night I heard the Nash start up and clatter down the blacktopped road. The wind came up and blew some rain against my window.

Papa didn't come home for a week.

* * *

I practiced roller skating on the porch. It was long and wide and smooth, except for a few places where the paint bubbled up and hadn't peeled yet. It was fun to pop the bubbles with the wheels. I only had to grab the railing three or four times and I was ready to try skating on the sidewalk.

To get to the sidewalk, I had to skate down our hill. I'd done it once or twice already; you just sit on the step, buckle on the skates, then pull up by the railing, bend your knees a little and let go. What a ride!

The big old maple at the bottom of the slope made a good stopper and kept me from sailing on into the street. It stung my hands a bit when I first hit, but I learned to push back at the same time, then real quick drag my foot and turn. It got so I could do it in one motion and be halfway down the block without skipping a beat.

Christmas vacation was over, it was 1935 and school had been back in a week. I never looked up *virgin* because Jake told me what it meant. My face must have looked like Mrs. Bowman's neck, and I never asked him another question for a month. Jake thought it was a scream and went around bragging how he knew and I didn't.

I finally cornered him in the lunchroom. "You bite your tongue, Jake Freeman!" I made my voice all low and growly like Susi's brother Roy. "Or see if you're my best friend anymore!" When I told him that, he shut up.

Mama always said, "Jake's a scamp, but his heart's in the right place."

I would grin and say, "I hope so!" And she would smile and flick water at me from the sprinkle bowl on the ironing board.

That day, I wore the brown flannel skirt Mama had made on her new machine and an old blue sweater. Papa had come home looking sorry and things had settled down a bit.

It had rained the night before and there were puddles here and there, but I wasn't afraid of getting wet, and I thought how it was fun to skate through puddles and watch the water spray in all directions.

I buckled on my skates and stood, got my balance and let go of the railing. Halfway down the hill I hit a puddle deeper than the others. It threw me off course a little and I missed the tree. Not by much. Just enough so I had to stretch real hard with one arm and catch hold of the trunk and swing around the other side. Only there wasn't any "other side." There was only a smelly old gray undershirt, a cement-hard chest, and two great grimy hands with dirt under the nails that pinched my shoulders something awful when I crashed.

Roy Cummings.

"Keep quiet," he growled and gave my shoulders a shake. "Are you all right?" He pushed me back a ways and looked me over like I might be dying and would bleed all over him.

I couldn't have made noise if I'd wanted too. The wind was knocked from my sails, as Papa would say, and I just wanted to breathe.

"Come on, Sis, easy does it." He waited till I could look him in the eye, then said, "Tell your papa I'm watching. And there will come a day, there surely will," and walked on down the street, hands shoved in the pockets of his dungarees, whistling "Yankee Doodle," cool as you please.

Chapter
Twelve

When I told Jake about Roy Cummings hiding behind the tree, he ran out front like he expected Roy to still be standing there. He wasn't, of course. Jake caught his breath, mumbled something about "what I'd like to do to that creep's face," and smashed his fist into the tree. The rough bark made his knuckles bleed and I thought how Jake would probably hurt himself worse than he could ever hurt Roy. But I had sense enough not to say it out loud.

Jake is older than me by nearly three years, but only one year ahead in school. That's because he started late, then flunked first grade. "It's not that he couldn't read if he wanted to," his teacher told Mrs. Freeman. "He just hasn't learned that he's in school to study, not to tease the girls."

Mrs. Freeman was telling me the story after Jake got his knuckles cleaned up and we were helping her bake chocolate cookies. Jake was supposed to scoop the hot cookies off the cookie sheet onto the bread wrapper to cool. Mrs. Freeman showed him how to rip it open and lay it out waxy side up so the cookies wouldn't stick. My job was to drop teaspoons of dough on a clean greased pan and put it in the oven.

Jake liked his cookies hot and I couldn't help but take a taste of dough now and then, so our jobs suited us just fine. The cookies didn't pile up very fast though.

When Mrs. Freeman got to the part about what Jake's father did when they got Jake's report card, she stopped the story, poured Jake and me each a big glass of milk, and sent us outside with two cookies apiece. "That's enough; you'll both be sick," she said, and set the latch hook on the screen door so the little ones couldn't get in. They set up a holler and Jake's second brother, Tim, tried to tackle him as we walked down the steps. Jake just moved out of his way and Mrs. Freeman settled them with the promise of "cookies and milk in fifteen minutes."

We ran through the break in the hedge and sat down behind the apple tree in my yard. The others weren't allowed in my yard without permission, so we could eat our cookies in peace.

I was laughing and breathless and trying not to choke on the crumbs when Jake grabbed my arm and spilt milk all down my best play dress. "If you tell anyone," he snapped at me, "I'll wring your neck."

I wanted to pop him. "What are you talking about? Jake Freeman, you ruined my dress!" I brushed the wet spot with the back of my hand, but it only made it worse. When I looked up, Jake's face was red as Chuckie's new scooter.

He looked away. "You know, the school thing." He picked up a dirt clod and threw it at Timmy who was inching his way through the hole in the hedge.

Jake missed and Tim scurried on back to their porch.

I wasn't too worried about Jake's threat. Papa said, "Jake's all bluster and bluff," and he was right, but I knew the school thing must bother him so I promised not to tell.

The fun was over though. I wanted to tell him, "It's all right. Nobody thinks you're stupid or anything. Lots of kids stay back a year in school." But Jake got all quiet and I wasn't sure it was the right thing to say.

We sat for a few more minutes listening to the blue jays' chatter and watching the clouds roll with the wind.

Sometimes we would sit like that for hours, Jake and me, and point out cloud shapes: animals and faces. Then we'd get to laughing and telling who they looked like and making up stories about that person until the picture changed and we could start all over again.

But that was mostly in the summer. It was colder now and the wind blew the clouds too fast. Anyway, Jake wasn't in the mood for cloud pictures or stories. He'd been acting different lately. Restless, like the neighbor's big old tomcat who prowled up and down the fence line whenever Millie was around.

"He wants her to come and play," Krista insisted when the tom started up his yowling. But usually Millie would just sit there on the porch licking a paw and pretend not to hear.

If the yowling got too loud, Mr. Freeman would come out and throw one of the kids' galoshes and tom would run off for a while.

Jake used to sit by me sometimes on the school bus. But lately he'd been sitting in the back with Bill Black and Eugene Wheeler. They'd get rowdy and loud and Mr. Carson, the bus driver, would tell them, "Sit down and be quiet or I'm gonna stop this bus and you can haul yourselves home."

They'd settle down then. Once I turned around and caught Jake staring at me. He smiled and winked, then turned back to his friends.

It was the same at school. We'd be talking and laughing, then Eugene would come along and punch his arm. "Come on, Freeman, Bill Boy's waiting." Then he'd wink at me, say, "See ya later, sweet cheeks," and drag Jake off with him.

"See ya, Cissy," Jake would laugh and go with him. I tried not to care, but it hurt my feelings. Then at home Jake would holler, "Meet me by the hedge in fifteen minutes." And for a while it would be like old times.

We talked about a lot of things. I could ask Jake anything and he always seemed to have the answer. Once, I asked him if he was scared to grow up. He shrugged and got a funny smile on his face. "Nah," he said, "why be scared about something you can't change?" He squatted on the ground and picked up a stick one of the little boys had been using for a gun.

I sat down cross-legged in front of him and stretched my skirt over my knees and feet. Jake moved away a little and started drawing circles in the dirt. "Are you?" he said out of the blue.

"What?"

"Scared of growing up."

I thought about it a minute. Jake had grown three inches in the last few months. I could tell because his pants were all too short. My own skirts fit the same as always, but I knew we weren't talking about clothes.

The truth is, I *was* scared. There had been so many changes. Papa drinking again, Mama crying all the time, Roy Cummings and his threats. I knew Roy wasn't all bluster and bluff. He meant business and he was mean. Roy Cummings gave me the creeps and I wasn't ashamed to say so. I had lots of friends, but none as close as Jake, and he was changing too. I'd been feeling sort of lost, like everyone had gone off somewhere and left me behind.

"Do you think I'm growing up too, Jake?" I didn't know why, but the idea made me feel warm inside, like a cup of cocoa on a frost-cold day.

Jake tossed the stick toward his back porch. He stood up and held out his hand. I grabbed it and he helped me up like always, but then he let go and just looked at me for the longest time. I didn't move a muscle. Somehow I thought it was important to stay still. I could usually tell what Jake was thinking, but the look on his face just then was a mystery.

Then Jake did the strangest thing. He reached out with one finger and pushed a strand of hair off my cheek and back behind my ear. "Yes," he said, so soft I could hardly hear him. "Yes, Cissy, you are growing up." And he turned right around, walked up the back porch steps and into his house without even saying "See you later" like he always did.

I thought then how if growing up could make a person act so strange, maybe it wasn't so great after all.

Chapter
Thirteen

Krista had a birthday the end of February. We had a real party with ice cream, sponge cake and licorice candy. And lots of presents.

Mama made her a navy blue cotton dress with a white, scalloped collar and a dark blue ribbon down the front. I saved my milk money for two weeks and bought her a paper doll cut-out book. She got a yo-yo and a roller hoop, and a Tousle-head Patsy Ann from Papa.

I never will forget Krista's face when she saw that doll. Not if I live to be a hundred. It came in a fancy box with extra clothes and a shiny heart bracelet hanging on its arm. And its dress was just like Krista's: navy blue polka dots with a wide, scalloped collar. It had soft blonde curls, sleepy eyes and a dimple in its chin.

Krista sure loved that doll. The smile came back into her eyes and she took it with her everywhere, except for school. Chuckie wasn't allowed near it. "Patsy Ann can take care of herself while I'm in school," she told him.

She propped Cecilia up on top of the chest of drawers, out of Chuckie's reach. Once in a while she would check to be sure Cecilia was still there, but Patsy Ann was Krista's doll-child now.

The bad things started happening in March, right after Baby Grace was born.

Such a pretty baby! Red-gold curls like Krista's, Chuckie's big brown eyes. Mama named her Grace for Grandma Eva's mother.

Great-Grandma had a gentle name, but fire in her spirit. I loved to listen to the stories of how Grandma Eva and her sisters were born in a covered wagon coming west to California. Her sisters, they were triplets, died, leaving only Grandma Eva. They never got to California. Stopped somewhere in Nevada and built a wood-log cabin.

Once Great-Grandma even chased off Indians. "Killed one too," Grandma Eva said, "not that she had aught against him. Just defending her home!" Mama came in then and stopped the story, saying how I was too young to hear it, and Grandma Eva passed away that spring so I never did get to hear it all.

Mama said how Baby Grace would need fire in her spirit. "To cope with this old world and all its trials," she said, and lay back on her pillow, white and tired.

Papa looked as white and tired as Mama. He took to coming home a different way each day. I know 'cause I was on the porch with Chuckie and Krista every evening for a week, shelling peas and folding diapers, keeping the little ones busy and out of Mama's hair. Mama had her hands full feeding Baby Grace and keeping her clean and all.

I saw Papa come home every night. One time from New Avenue, the next from California Boulevard. Once I even spied the Nash turn in from Baxter Lane. He would eat his supper, check on Mama and the baby, then go out again till late at night.

One night Papa came home from Keyhole Nelson's Bar. I know 'cause he smelled like smoke and whiskey. He wasn't being careful and he stepped on Tarzan's tail.

Poor Tarzan yowled loud enough to scare a ghost. Krista

screamed and followed him underneath the table, moaning how Papa had killed her kitty. Mama said, "Now you've woke the baby," and Chuckie bit Papa on the leg. I don't know what got into him. Chuckie never bit anyone before. I guess he thought Papa had killed the kitty too, and everyone was upset and he just couldn't help it.

Papa hit him. Smacked him right in the face with the back of his hand. Slit a gash in Chuckie's cheek with his knuckle. Mama almost fainted. The doctor had to come and give him stitches.

Papa sat down on the kitchen floor and cried.

* * *

Two days later, I saw Roy Cummings leaning on the fence-post at the corner of the house across the street. It was after school, and I was walking home. He grinned at me and tipped his hat—an old fedora that looked like he'd dug it from the city dump. I could see the back right fender of the Nash sticking out of the shack and I knew Papa was home.

I ran in the house and went to tell Papa that Roy Cummings was there, 'cause I was scared he might come to the door. But Papa was in his room with Mama and Baby Grace, and the door was shut and I knew I shouldn't bother them.

Maybe if I'd have bothered them, things would have turned out different. Papa could have got away, or hid in the closet.

As it was, the doorbell rang ten minutes later. I was halfway to the door when Papa got there. I didn't have a chance to do a thing.

"Are you Charles Summers?" one policeman asked and showed his shiny badge.

Papa's shoulders drooped and his hands started to shake. I could see them dangling at his sides. He nodded yes, and the policeman came in the door. "Put your hands up and turn around," he said. "You're under arrest for grand larceny and embezzlement."

I couldn't breathe. Just stood there quiet and watched them take him away. My papa, in handcuffs with a metal chain, going off to jail in a police car.

I heard Mama gasp. She was standing right behind me. Baby Grace must have been asleep in the buggy. "I knew it," Mama whispered, "I knew it sure as I was born." She turned and went back to their room and shut the door. I heard her sobbing and let her be.

*   *   *

Chuckie fell asleep on the rag rug by his bed. He looked so sweet curled up in a ball, his little cheek pressed against his hand and Tarzan cuddled underneath his chin.

Krista was in the kitchen sharing pretend tea with Patsy Ann. They'd already had supper, so I left them and went and climbed the apple tree. A person could think up there with only the birds and sky for company.

The shadows were already creeping around Mr. Johnson's chicken coop in the yard behind us.

Dotty Johnson was my best friend, out of all the girls anyway. She had been the first one to say hello when school started right after we moved. Then we discovered that she lived behind me and if I climbed the apple tree and she sat on the roof of the chicken coop, we could send signals back and forth with pieces of glass from her mother's broken hand mirror. Of course, the sun had to be bright to do it.

It wasn't bright now. The evening light was fading fast and Dotty would be in her bedroom doing homework.

A scrawny hen flapped across the yard and chased a robin-redbreast away from the worm he was scratching up for supper. I wanted to throw a rock at that old hen. The papa robin had a family to feed; I could hear the babies screeching from their nest in the Freemans' elm tree. But all the rocks were on the ground and I didn't feel like climbing down just then.

Instead, I asked God to please be sure my papa got some supper and, if it wasn't too much trouble, help him come home before Easter.

I'd no sooner said, "Amen" when I felt the tree limb shake. Jake was down there tugging on the end of the branch. The soft fuzzy twigs had just begun to show green and a few of the buds came off in his hand.

"Come on down, Cissy," he said and pushed the branch aside. "It's almost dark and Krista said to tell you Chuckie's up."

He was right. The shadows were gone now and the whole sky had faded to a gray-green sheet. The light in the bedroom snapped on and I could see Chuckie's nose pressed against the window. Krista stood behind him rocking Patsy Ann.

I shimmied down the tree and brushed the bark off my legs.

Jake pulled a twig off the apple branch and threw it against the back fence. We both just stood there quiet for a while, then Jake said, "Sorry about your papa, Cissy."

I nodded and went back in the house.

Chapter
Fourteen

I didn't see Jake much that spring. What with all that happened to my family we couldn't meet in the afternoons. At school he still hung around with Eugene and Billy and their friends. Most of them would turn away when I walked by and pretend not to see me.

My friend Dotty said to never mind. "They just don't know what to say, Cissy. No one else's father has ever been in jail."

I thought how my papa shouldn't be in jail either. I didn't know whether to be angry or ashamed. I was always afraid, but I didn't tell anyone. Not even Jake.

* * *

It scared me bad when one of the hall monitors came into class one day and interrupted Mrs. Cruger's geography lesson.

"I got a note for Cissy Summers from the principal," he said so the whole class could hear. "Please give it to her before time to go home."

Mrs. Cruger frowned and read the note. "Thank you, I'll take care of it," she said, and stuck the folded white paper in the pocket of her dress. She didn't even look at me. Just turned back to the blackboard and went on with the lesson.

The girl who sat in front of me whispered something to

Dotty. Dotty reached across the aisle and punched her in the arm, and some of the others started to whisper and giggle.

"That will be quite enough." Mrs. Cruger slapped the eraser down on the railing so hard it made the dust fly. We all sat up and paid attention.

I knew I wouldn't get the note till after school.

Dotty offered to wait and walk me home. "No," I said, "go catch the bus, I don't mind walking alone." It wasn't all that far and I didn't know what the note would say. I wondered if I was in trouble, but couldn't think of anything I'd done wrong.

As it was, I caught the bus anyway. Mrs. Cruger just put the note in an envelope and wrote *Mrs. Summers* on the outside. "This is for your mother, Cissy," she said and handed it over. "Please give it to her tonight."

"And Cissy," she called as I headed out the door, "tell your mama if there is anything I can do, please let me know."

I nodded yes. Lots of people had said that since Papa got arrested. Some ladies from church brought cakes and potato salad. They came over every day at first.

"You'd think we were having a funeral," Mama sniffed. But I know she was grateful for the food. Krista and Chuckie and I were thankful too; Mama's friend from Sunday school made the best chocolate cake in town.

I guess I shouldn't have read the note. It was addressed to Mama, but Mrs. Cruger didn't seal the envelope, and anyway, if I had to be embarrassed in class I should at least know what it was all about.

"Dear Mrs. Summers," it said, "We find that we have more than enough volunteers to chaperone the May Day celebration, and we feel that under the circumstances someone else should take your place. I'm sure you understand." It was signed by our principal's wife and head of the entertainment committee.

I thought it just as well, because Mama was so tired lately

and had enough to do with Krista and Chuckie and the new baby.

Mama read the note, but instead of looking happy to be relieved from duty, her lips got tight and her cheeks got red—like when she was mad at Papa and wouldn't give him the satisfaction of making a fuss.

She crumpled the note into a tiny ball and threw it in the trash. "Well, I guess I know who my friends are," was all she said as she dished up some of the chicken stew Dotty's mother had sent over.

* * *

We didn't go to church that Easter. Actually, we hadn't gone much at all since Papa went to jail, but it was the first time I remember ever staying home at Easter.

"The baby's too little, Cissy," Mama explained. "Besides, I haven't had time to make you or Krista anything decent to wear."

I thought how she used to tell us: "We go to church to worship, not to show off. God doesn't care what we wear." That was back in Pike when Papa was let go from the bank and my good white organdy dress got a stain. Mama picked a lily from the plant beside the porch and pinned it on the bodice. "There now," she said and twisted the stem so it didn't stab me in the eye, "the stain hardly shows. You look pretty as a garden flower, doesn't she, Charles?"

I don't remember what Papa said back. I just remember Mama polished all our shoes and put new paper in the bottom of Papa's old good boots. She dusted off her blue felt hat and ironed the veil. I guess we looked just as good as anyone else that Easter.

But this year Mama didn't even try.

* * *

Krista started coughing around the first of May. Mama

thought she had a cold. Next thing we knew she was throwing up and couldn't breathe good.

The doctor came for three days straight. On May the third, at four o'clock that afternoon, he came out of Krista's room and closed the door. He took Mama's hand and said, "I'm sorry, Mrs. Summers, there was nothing I could do," and shook his head.

Mama screamed and ran into the bedroom. The doctor said to leave her be, and that's when I told God he could have Baby Grace if he'd give us Krista back.

"The Lord giveth, and the Lord taketh away." That's what Mrs. Goodwin had said when Judy Thomas's mother had a baby and her grandmother passed on the next day.

"But Judy's grandmother was old," I told God that day. "Krista's only seven, and if it's all the same to you, we'll take her back and you can have Baby Grace."

It's not that I didn't love Baby Grace. She was sweet and soft and fun to cuddle when she lay real quiet and smelled okay, but I loved Krista better.

God didn't give Krista back.

Mama died too, May third of 1935. Oh, she kept on walking and talking and sometimes even sang, "Jesus loves me, this I know," to Baby Grace. But something inside her went away with Krista, and it never came back.

Chapter
Fifteen

I liked the wild, protected spot at the corner of the porch. It was thick with jasmine, hyacinth and rose of Sharon. I could crawl way deep inside, right up against the house where there was room enough to sit with my knees drawn up and read and dream. No one else knew about my hiding place. Not even Jake. That made it better than the apple tree.

I read part of *The Good Earth* that summer. Mama had said, "No. It isn't fit for young ladies, especially if they're almost thirteen," but I read it anyway 'cause it was big and thick and I could get lost in the story all summer if I stretched it out.

It was easy to stretch it out. What with Chuckie to help take care of and Baby Grace to do for, I had a busy summer.

People asked us how we were, Mama and me. Mama always said, "We're doing fine, thank you," then shut the door and went off to her room with one of her headaches. I tried not to say anything. I didn't want to talk to people and lie and tell them, "I'm fine," when I really wanted Papa and Krista back. That's why I liked my hiding place.

* * *

Jake and I were together only once that summer. Mrs. Freeman said how she was worried about Jake's grandpa. He didn't

Chapter Fifteen

own a telephone and she hadn't heard from him in weeks. She
asked would Jake run over and check on him? And she offered
to watch Chuckie and the baby so I could go too.

"It'll do the child good to get out of that house awhile," I
heard her tell Mr. Freeman. "Goodness knows, her mother can't
manage, poor thing."

So Jake and I took the streetcar clear across town to visit
Grandpa Freeman.

Grandpa's house was in a rundown neighborhood of wooden
shacks with curled tin roofs and sagging doors. It had a living
room, sleeping room and dining room all in one, and a tiny
kitchen no bigger than Mr. Johnson's chicken coop. The place
was cluttered with books and papers and junk that Grandpa
Freeman called "antiques." My favorite was a big brass cowbell.
It hung on the wall over a cold wood stove next to a picture of
Jake's Grandma Jess.

Grandpa seemed healthy as ever when he met us at the door
and we handed over the pumpkin cake Mrs. Freeman had sent
for his dinner. "You two keep out of this," Mrs. Freeman had
warned us. "Lord knows that man gets little enough to eat."

She needn't have worried. Grandpa Freeman never offered
us any cake. He set it on the sink and settled down to reminisc-
ing about his farm in Arkansas and the cow who wore that bell.

"That cow's name was Matilda," Grandpa said, "and she
didn't have a lick of sense." He stopped to pack some sweet
tobacco in his pipe. "Matilda was a pretty cow," he chuckled,
"and she sure could turn old Samson's head."

Jake looked bored, like he'd heard the story a hundred times.
But I hadn't, so I flashed him a look that said be quiet and
asked, "Who was Samson, Grandpa Freeman?"

Grandpa took a long pull from his pipe. "Well now, Samson
was the biggest ornery, cantankerous old bull we ever had on
the place. 'Tilda was the only cow could ever tame him. Sure as

heck no human ever could. Why, I remember the time that randy old cuss took a notion to . . ."

Grandpa couldn't finish his story because Jake took a coughing fit right in the middle. I thought how it sounded fake; he never had a cold or anything before we got there, but he coughed so hard it made Grandpa take notice. He looked at Jake real close, then looked at me.

"Now let's see," he said, tapping his pipe in the ashtray, "we were talking about Matilda."

I wanted to remind him we weren't talking about Matilda just then, we were talking about Samson, but I was afraid to interrupt or we'd never hear the whole story about either one.

Jake got better all at once, and Grandpa Freeman went on. "Jake's Grandma Jess had a fondness for petunias, rest her soul. Trouble was, so did Matilda." He settled deeper into his chair cushion.

"Jess had a flower box right next to the back porch where she planted the prettiest petunias you ever saw. They got big as saucers, and by midsummer that flower bed looked like a pile of silk ribbons and smelled like sunshine on clover.

"It was just too tempting for Matilda. Every morning that heifer would graze her way over to the fence line, paw the ground and bellow like she'd just dropped a calf. If I went into the pasture she'd follow me back to the gate and try to push past me into the yard. It got so I had to pick me a switch to keep her back.

"One morning Jess went out to scatter corn for the hens and found Matilda smack dab in the middle of the flower bed, eyes closed and chewing cud like she was in cow heaven. There wasn't a petunia to be found. That cussed cow ate every scrap: stems, leaves and all."

Grandpa took a deep breath. "They must have heard Jess screaming all the way over to Milford County. I never saw her so mad before or since. I think she would have butchered Matilda then and there if I hadn't promised on my life it would never happen again.

"I had to nail the gate shut and build another on the other side of the pasture by the road. Then I bought the biggest, loudest dang cowbell I could find and wired it to that critter's neck. You could hear her coming for miles.

"Matilda hated that bell. Spent a week trying to rub it off. Samson loved it, though; followed her around everywhere till that poor old cow was just too tuckered out to look for flowers."

By this time Jake was rolling his eyes and tapping his foot and I knew he was itching to go, but I just had to ask one more question.

"Did they ever make up, Grandpa Freeman? Your Jess and Matilda, I mean."

Grandpa looked strange then, sort of sad even though he smiled. "You know, it's funny," he said. "Jess cried for two solid hours, then took herself outside and carried a whole basket of sweet clover to that cow. By the time I finished building the new gate, she was petting Matilda's nose and telling her, 'Sorry I yelled at you 'Tilda.' "

Then Grandpa pushed himself out of his chair and shuffled to the hot plate by the sink to pour some coffee. "Never did understand that woman," he whispered, "never in sixty-some years, God rest her soul."

"I like Grandpa Freeman," I told Jake on the way home. "Do you think he'd want to be my grandpa too?"

I didn't mean for real, of course, but Jake must have thought I did 'cause he just gave me a funny look and didn't answer.

Chapter
Sixteen

One morning in September, Mama went to bed with a head-ache and never got back up. I gave Chuckie lunch and supper and helped him feed Tarzan. That kitten was now a cat full grown and Mama wouldn't let him in the house because of Baby Grace. "He might try to suck the milk," she said.

"Why?" I asked, and really meant it.

"That's what cats do," she said. "They smell milk on the baby's mouth and lick it. He might smother her."

She shooed me off and turned back to her sewing machine. She had started a dress for Krista, and wanted to finish it and one for me for the next school year. She finished Krista's dress in August. I wanted to ask her why, because it was way too small for me, and Krista didn't need it in heaven, but I didn't ask.

Mama had been doing strange things lately and I'd given up trying to understand. Like her talks with Papa. We only got one letter from him after his arrest. Mama read it out loud. He said for Mama not to come and see his disgrace, and "Tell my Pumpkins I love them and didn't mean to hurt them, or you either, Lynetta. I just wanted life to be better for us, you know?"

I tried to call him after Krista went to heaven, but the lady on the phone said he couldn't talk now and to call back later. When I did, they said he wasn't taking phone calls, and the post office returned my letter after three whole weeks, NO FOR-WARDING ADDRESS stamped in big red letters all across the front.

Mama talked to him just the same. "Now, Charles," I heard her say one day when I was trying to find a safety pin for Baby Grace's diaper, "Krista needs new shoes for school and I have to finish Cissy's dress. Will you take Krista into town this afternoon? And get some socks for Chuckie, if you can. He's worn the ones he has clear through and I can't darn them one more stitch!"

She did have some things right. Chuckie needed socks real bad. At least he would for winter. He could get by barefoot only another month or so.

When I came back to her door an hour later she was quiet, sitting up in bed with a sweater on her shoulders like it wasn't ninety degrees outside.

"Mama?" I asked, "are you all right?"

She smiled at me, but wouldn't talk. I spent the evening tending little ones and being scared for Mama and sad for Papa and mad for Krista, all three at once.

* * *

We might have made it if Baby Grace had not got sick.

By the morning of my birthday on September second, Mama still wouldn't talk to anyone but Papa. She wouldn't get out of bed or tend the baby or nothing.

School was to start up in one more week and I wondered what I'd do if she wasn't well by then. I thought to call the doctor but he was at another house and couldn't come, and I was sure Mama wasn't really sick. Just tired, that's all.

Chuckie had got up and made some pancakes—the batter anyway. He had watched Mama and me make pancakes a hundred times or more, even helped a couple of times. This time he'd really done a half-good job, except for flour all over the counter and a dropped egg on the floor underneath my chair. How it got all the way over there I'll never know. I heated up the grill and added some more milk to the flour and eggs, and some baking powder to make it rise.

With Chuckie settled to the table, dripping syrup down his shirt with every bite, I thought I'd better check on Baby Grace. She hadn't cried yet this morning and Mama always said, "Never wake a sleeping baby," so I'd left her be.

She was still asleep when I peeked into her buggy. But her breath sounded sort of rasping, like Krista's had before she died, and her skin looked sunburn red. I touched her cheek and about burnt my hand.

My heart thudded in my chest like it wanted to jump out on the floor. What if God had heard my prayer and took back Baby Grace? I didn't want that anymore, 'cause I knew Krista was fine in heaven, and Baby Grace belonged right here.

"Oh, please, please, God, don't let our baby die," I cried, carrying her to Mama.

I shook Mama's shoulder until she opened her eyes, then handed her the baby. "She's hot, Mama, Baby Grace is sick." I didn't know what to do. Mama smiled and rocked and sang, "Jesus loves me, this I know." But she didn't try to wake her up or cool her skin or give her medicine like she'd done for Krista.

"Chuckie?" I screamed real loud, "Chuckie, you come here right now!"

I could hear his plate hit the linoleum and break and his little bare feet squashing on the hardwood floor as he ran. I could hear Papa's clock going tick tick tick, real slow from the dresser across the room. I could hear Mama start to hum "Amazing Grace," and Baby's breath hissing in and out, in and out. I could hear my own heart pound in rhythm with the worker's hammer on the roof next door, and I could hear a blue jay scolding from the birdbath in the neighbor's yard.

I picked up Chuckie and sat him on the bed. "Stay here," I said, and gave him a shake to be sure he listened. A tear dripped down his syrup-sticky face. I pretended not to see. "Don't move, you hear? And don't let Mama drop the baby."

Then I ran. Out the back door. Through the break in the hedge. Around the washtub on the lawn, past the empty rabbit hutch, up the back steps and into Mrs. Freeman's kitchen without a knock or a "May I please come in?"

Chapter
Seventeen

Mrs. Freeman came. The doctor came. A lady came to talk to
Mama. But Mama wouldn't talk. She just sat and smiled and
I knew she was talking to Papa in her head again.

The lady took Baby Grace. I screamed and tried to grab her
back, but Mrs. Freeman held my shoulders hard, then let me
cry a while till I calmed down.

"The baby's going to be fine, child," she said when I would
listen. "She has the croup, that's all. Babies get croup all the
time. Why, all my young'uns had it at least twice before they
turned two!"

She sent Chuckie over to play with Jake's little brothers.
Mama didn't like him to go over there too often. "Those Freeman children are wild," she'd said. But Mama wasn't saying
anything just then and I thought how it wouldn't hurt to have
him somewhere else awhile.

"I'll keep him till suppertime," Mrs. Freeman said, and
smiled. I knew she wanted to be kind. "You get your wits together and your mama settled. That social worker will be back.

"Best see to this mess too," she clucked her tongue as she
hustled out the kitchen door.

Jake helped. Which was nice of him, seeing how I hadn't

been very friendly all that summer. He just pitched in and mopped up egg and syrup and never said a word. I was glad for that.

* * *

The social lady came back the next morning with the doctor. Mrs. Freeman held my shoulders as they took Mama away. "She's going to a nice place, child, clean and all, where she can rest and get well."

The doctor said Baby Grace was doing better. The social lady said how it was best I didn't see her just now and to pack my clothes and Chuckie's and she'd be back to get us in the afternoon. "Mrs. Freeman here will help you," she smiled and climbed into the car with Mama.

I thought, "Why should Mrs. Freeman help?"

"Why do I have to pack?" I said out loud. "I can look after Chuckie until Baby Grace is well and Mama's ready to come home."

Mrs. Freeman wouldn't meet my eye and I knew there was trouble coming sure. "You can't stay here by yourself, child, it's against the law. They'll find someone nice to care for you until your mama's well."

She looked across the yard to Chuckie and three or four other little ones playing on her front porch. "Land, child, I'd take you if I could, but I got too many of my own to care for."

* * *

"They can't make me go," I told Tarzan. "Never in a million years!" I crawled into the jasmine and pushed him to a cat-sized spot underneath the rose of Sharon. He yawned and opened one green eye, but otherwise didn't bother to move. He'd taken a liking to my spot that summer; it was cool and dark, a perfect place for naps. I didn't mind much, long as he kept to himself and let me read.

I didn't have a book that afternoon. The air smelled thick and smokey and the sun had burned the grass to brown. Even the starlings and the blue jays hid in bushes and the branches of Jake's avocado tree, waiting for evening to come and cool the day. *The Good Earth* lay where I'd left it underneath the mattress on my bed. It made a space wide as my fist between the box springs and the mattress, but Mama hadn't changed the sheets in weeks, so it was safe.

Chuckie found me. Crawled in like he'd known my hiding place forever. His soft blond curls all damp with sweat, his face and fingers sticky from the lollipop tucked between his teeth and cheek. "Want some?" he held it out for me to see. "It's cherry, Cissy. You like cherry?"

"I like cherry." I nodded and took a pretend lick.

When Chuckie grinned, the world lit up like nighttime in the city or Fourth of July on the beach, all sparkling and exciting and real. The pink scar on his cheek, where Papa hit him, puckered like a fat crawly worm when he smiled. I wanted to take him in the house and clean it off, but scars like that don't just wash away.

He must have seen my eyes just then because his smile stopped. "Tell me a story, Cissy, please?" He pushed his way into my lap, taking down a whole clump of jasmine where anyone could see. "Tell me a story where the papa doesn't go away, and the mama gets well, and the sister gets tired of heaven and comes home 'cause she forgot her Cecilia and her Patsy Ann!"

I didn't know what to say. I couldn't tell a story like that 'cause I knew we both wanted it to be true and it would never be. Never again.

Then I remembered Mrs. Goodwin's story about heaven.

When Judy Thomas's grandma died, Mrs. Goodwin told the whole class about heaven. I remembered it when Grandma Eva died and again when God took Krista—it was what made me feel better when I got too lonesome or sad for them.

So I told Chuckie about the streets of gold and pearly gates. I told how everyone was happy there and sang songs with the angels, and nothing there could hurt you and no one ever cried.

"There'll be no reason for tears," Mrs. Goodwin had said, "because Jesus is there, and he takes care of all his children."

I hope Chuckie understood. He looked up at me with eyes as wide and round as china buttons. Then we heard Mrs. Freeman call.

"Cissy? Cissy, child, where are you? Come on now, it's not polite to keep the social worker waiting."

She was standing right next to the hyacinth and there was nowhere for me to run, especially with Chuckie on my lap.

Chapter
Eighteen

The social lady took us to St. Stephen's Orphanage, an ugly brown stucco building with thick cement steps and heavy double doors. She pulled the cord hanging from a rafter on the covered porch and a deep BONG came from somewhere inside the house. It sounded just like the old grandfather clock Grandma Eva used to keep in her parlor.

After what seemed like an hour, one of the doors swung open and a lady dressed in a black robe with a big white collar led us down a wide hallway. My shoes made clicking noises on the hardwood floor. I thought how maybe I should tiptoe 'cause the house was so quiet, but then we turned a corner and the floor had carpet on it.

They let us stay together for a week. Chuckie and me, I mean. Baby Grace was still in the hospital and didn't get there for a while. When she did, they put her in the nursery.

St. Stephen's was a foundling home. They didn't have a school and there really was no place for a girl my age. Our first day there they tried to take Chuckie to the boy's ward without me. They changed their minds quick when he set up a howl that could rattle your teeth.

Sister Veronica pursed her lips and scowled, but she let him climb back on my lap. "He'll be fine in a day or two," she said. "Children his age are always frightened at first."

Sister Veronica was the Mother Superior at the orphanage. She was short and round with a beaver smile and big front teeth that bit into her lower lip whenever she closed her mouth. The other sisters called her Reverend Mother. I just called her Ma'am and tried not to stare.

Now she handed me two blankets and a pile of clothes. "See he puts these on," she said, and led us down the hall to the dorm.

She unlocked the door with a long brass key. The hinges squeaked when she pushed it open. It gave me the chills—that and the fact that the room was cold as the middle of January. It was clean, though, and smelled like floor wax and fresh-ironed sheets.

Sister Veronica pointed to the far end of the room. "There are two cots against that wall," she said. "You can sleep next to him for a few days." Then she put her finger under my chin. "But mind now," she scolded, "only a day or two, then he has to follow the rules." She shook her head and swished out of the room without explaining any of the rules she wanted us to follow.

We found out soon enough.

The room was long and skinny with child-size cots along both walls. There was a bathroom with two sinks clear down at the end next to our beds, but the door was always locked and you had to ring a bell if you needed to use it. I guess that was all right for the little ones, but it sure made my life a misery.

In the morning Sister Veronica marched down the room, unlocked the bathroom door and rang a big brass cowbell.

That bell made me sit up and take notice. It was exactly like the one Jake's grandpa had. I'd seen it just three weeks before, but it all seemed so long ago. That visit to Grandpa Freeman's was the last time I talked to Jake before Grace got sick and they took us all away.

l rubbed some sleep sand from my eyes and realized Chuckie and I were the only ones still in bed. Ten other boys about Chuckie's age stood at the end of their beds. They each held a towel, wash rag and a toothbrush. No one said a thing, but they looked at us like we were from the moon.

Sister Veronica handed Chuckie a towel and motioned for him to stand up like the others. Chuckie looked at me, then moved when he saw I was getting up too.

"You will help me supervise the children, Cissy. Then you may use my quarters to wash."

She rang the bell again, took Chuckie by the shoulders and turned him so that he was first in line. Then she led the way into the bathroom.

Half an hour later, everyone but me had washed and dressed. Sister Veronica looked at the watch she wore on a chain around her neck. "Fifteen minutes, children," she announced, and all the boys scrambled to tie their shoes and smooth the covers on their beds.

"Come with me, Cissy Marie." She handed me a skirt and blouse from a bundle she had under her arm and walked out of the room. I could hear Chuckie sniffle as I turned to follow, but I smiled to tell him, "It's okay," and another boy came over to show him how to tuck his blanket in. I knew he'd be all right for a while.

After I washed and dressed, we all went into chapel. There were eleven boys, counting Chuckie, which seemed to upset Anne, a younger lady in a gray jumper and white blouse, who nodded yes and bowed whenever the other sisters spoke to her. "The number isn't even," I heard her tell Sister Veronica. "How can they walk two by two if the number isn't even?" Then came the little girls—six of them, all younger than Krista was before she died. Chuckie had to sit with the other boys while I sat in back with Anne.

In chapel everyone else knew what to do. At first I tried to follow the others as they stood up, sat down, knelt and waved their arms, but finally I just gave up and watched. I couldn't understand what anyone was saying. I found out later they were talking Latin, saying prayers I'd never learned.

"I learned a prayer in Sunday school," I told Anne. She frowned and put her finger to her lips to tell me to hush.

After lunch, Anne led me to Sister Veronica's office. "Reverend Mother wants to see you," was all she said, but her face was serious and her eyes looked frightened, like a raccoon kit I found once in a field close to my school in Pike. I wanted to pick it up and take it home, the poor lost thing, but my teacher said to leave it be.

"That coon's not lost, Cissy," she told me. "Its mama's probably hiding in those bushes over there, scared to death you're going to hurt her baby."

Sure enough, when we went back to the sidewalk and stood as still as stones, that mother coon scrambled out of the bushes, picked up her kit by the back of its neck and lit out for kingdom come.

I wondered if the look in Anne's eyes meant I should be frightened too. But Sister Veronica wasn't so bad. In fact I liked her even though she was stricter than Mama ever thought of being. Then I thought how maybe Mama had come for me and Anne was only acting so she wouldn't spoil the surprise. I had to try hard not to run ahead of her down the hall.

But Mama wasn't in the room. Just Sister Veronica, who sat behind a huge, brown desk tapping her fingers on the blotter.

"Cissy," she said when I stood in front of her, "we have a problem."

She was quiet for so long I thought maybe she expected me to tell her what the problem was.

"Don't fidget," she finally said. "Stand up straight."

She stood up and walked over to the window. There was a long row of steps leading down to the sidewalk and a paved road with a few cars going up and down. A streetcar track ran right down the middle and I knew we must be on a main street somewhere.

I hadn't paid attention when the social lady brought us here. My eyes had been sore from crying and I was trying to keep Chuckie busy, so I didn't know where we were. I thought it best not to ask just then.

Sister Veronica sighed, like Mama did when Papa went away and finally came home again, sick and sorry he'd ever been born.

"We didn't know that you weren't, ah . . . of the church, Cissy," she said. "The woman who brought you here just assumed . . . Oh, well," she sighed again, "we'll just have to make the best of it."

She straightened some papers on the desk and sat back down. She didn't give me permission to sit, so I stayed where I was and wondered, *Make the best of what?*

"You'll have to learn your rosary and Hail Mary, but you won't be here very long."

"Yes, ma'am," I said then, "but I did learn one prayer in Sunday school."

Most of the time I prayed inside my head and just told God whatever I wanted him to know, but I wanted to please Sister Veronica, so I started reciting: "Our Father who art in heaven, hallowed be thy name . . ."

I hadn't got so far as "Thy kingdom come" when Sister interrupted me.

"That's a good start, Cissy, but there are others you should learn. St. Mary's has a catechism on Sunday mornings; you'll go there while you're with us. But I'm afraid we'll have to find another place for you. We only care for babies here."

I put my hands behind my back so she couldn't see them

shaking. "Yes, ma'am," I said, "but Chuckie and I won't need to be here long." I felt better just saying it. "As soon as Mama and Baby Grace get well, we'll all go home again."

Sister Veronica looked like she'd just been spooked by a mouse. She bent her head to scrub at a water ring on the desk. When she'd rubbed it clean, she went to the door and called Anne to come and take me to the day room.

"We'll talk again, Cissy, very soon," she said and shooed me out the door.

Chapter
Nineteen

We'd been at St. Stephen's for about three weeks when the car showed up again. I'd seen it parked out front the day we came, all shiny black with three sets of windows and clean, white tires. It came again the day they brought Baby Grace home from the hospital.

She was bundled in a blanket, all pink and smelling good. I got to hold her before they took her to the nursery. She smiled at me, the sweetest smile, and waved her arms and made little gurgling sounds. If I'd known what they were planning, I would have held her longer.

I was supposed to polish the benches in the entrance hall, but I couldn't resist looking out the window. I watched awhile every day and made up stories in my head about how Mama would come walking up the street, her hand tucked nice and cozy under Papa's arm. They'd laugh and talk until they reached the steps, then run up to the door in a hurry to see us. "We've come to take you home, Cissy," they'd say, and they'd cry and hug me close. Papa would ruffle my hair and call me his little Pumpkin and say, "Go fetch your brother while Mama gets the baby." We'd all go home again to the house on York Street and I'd run to the hedge and holler for Jake and tell him all about St.

Stephen's, like I'd just been away for a long visit.

But this day I didn't get Mama and Papa as far as the steps before the black car pulled up out front. A man in a gray jacket, black cap and shiny boots got out and opened the back door. Another man stepped out and turned to help a lady over the curb.

Later I would remember the way the sunlight caught the glimmer of the ruby on her finger. How her bright red nails rested against the sleeve of her husband's navy blue jacket, and how her hand trembled when she brought it for a moment to her painted mouth.

Was she nervous? Afraid? Or just excited to know she'd soon have two babies to love? Two babies that belonged to me.

She had no right. No right to them at all.

It dawned on me, when Uncle Edward asked me later, that I could not remember her face. Not if you boiled me in oil and fed me to the cannibals. I never did remember what Chuckie and Grace's new mother looked like.

Before I thought to go get Anne or Sister Veronica to tell them we had visitors, they both came rushing down the hall. Anne ran the last few steps and took my arm. "Hurry, Cissy," she huffed, all out of breath. "We have things to see to in the day room." She pushed me right on by Sister Veronica, who made shooing motions with one hand and fanned her face with the other.

I wondered, was Chuckie sick? So I ran to keep up with Anne. I didn't have a choice anyway, 'cause she hung onto my arm like she thought I was going to turn a somersault in the hall.

When we got to the day room no one was there. It looked nice and tidy. Most of the little ones were down for their afternoon naps, and I'd already straightened it up after morning play time. We'd been taught first thing not to talk till we were spoken to, but I couldn't understand why Anne dragged me here. If Chuckie were sick or something had happened to Baby Grace, they would be in the infirmary.

Anne looked like she was standing barefoot on hot tar. She twisted and turned and shifted from one foot to the other in a fret.

She finally grabbed a box down from the highest shelf. "Here, Cissy. These dolls need washing. Get a rag from the storeroom and don't come out until they're nice and clean."

Those dolls were a mess. There were three of them with yellow yarn for hair, shoe-button eyes, and sackcloth bodies stuffed with beans. Two of them had only one eye each, and most of the hair had been ripped off the third. They were so dirty, I thought how it would take six years to get them clean.

Anne rushed out and I was tempted to follow her. I smelled a rat and not the kind with fur. In the first place, Anne was too upset to care about a bunch of dolls. And anyway, there were four brand-new rubber ones just like Krista's Patsy Ann that a rich lady had donated to St. Stephen's just the week before. The same lady from the car, I'd bet.

I struggled with my conscience. Anne had told me to stay here and clean the dolls. But if Chuckie or Grace were in trouble, they needed *me,* not a bunch of strangers.

I peeled off my shoes and socks and peeked around the day room door. Anne was nowhere in sight, and the door to the infirmary just down the hall was closed. I tiptoed past the boys' dorm room. One of the little ones coughed and I could hear the rustle of the monitor's robe as she got up from her chair to check on him.

There would be someone watching in the nursery too.

By the-time I worked my way to the end of the hall and turned toward the infirmary, I felt sick enough to need it for myself.

Chapter Nineteen

I pressed my ear against the door and listened. No one was crying in there, or coughing and sneezing either. In fact it was quiet as the chapel at suppertime. I got up the nerve to try the door, but it was locked and the handle wouldn't even turn. I gave up and scooted back to the day room.

I'd got through scrubbing two dolls when Anne hustled back into the room and said how I could stop now and wash my hands and comb my hair because "Reverend Mother wants to see you in the office."

The vinegar water had turned the dolls a muddy brown, but Anne didn't seem to notice. She just packed them up wet as they were and stuck the box back on the shelf.

When Anne led me to the office, the big black car was gone. She sort of pushed me into the room, and I could hear her sob as she ran back to the entrance hall.

Chapter
Twenty

I knew there was trouble when Sister told me to sit down. No one ever sat in Sister's office, unless it was a visitor from outside.

"Cissy," she said, "your brother and the baby have gone to stay with a very nice family." She held up her hand to say be quiet, but she didn't have to; I couldn't even think what she was saying, let alone talk about it.

"They'll be well taken care of. These people have wanted a family for a long time. They will be good parents to Charles and Grace."

Good parents?

"What about Mama and Papa?" I couldn't help it. I had to ask out loud.

Sister didn't scold me for talking. "Your parents know all about it, child," was all she said to me. She said plenty to Uncle Edward later.

Sister Veronica walked over to the window and pulled back the drape. She breathed in deep like she needed some fresh air, but the evening had turned chilly and the window was closed. "I'm sorry, Cissy," she said without looking at me. "They could only take the little ones."

Chapter Twenty

I understood. No one wanted me except to help with chores because I was "too old to be cute, too young to be a wife, and too much responsibility, being thirteen and all." That's what some of the sisters had said. Behind my back, of course, but I heard.

I could see the color coming on the maple trees across the street. People strolling down the sidewalk had on sweaters or stoles.

"It's nippy out tonight," I heard Papa say, like he did in late September every year. "We're in for an early winter." But every year it would turn warm again and winter wouldn't really come till almost Christmas time.

Mama called it Indian Summer. It was always my favorite time of year. The maple leaves turned red and yellow, and we grew fat, orange pumpkins in the dirt patch behind the shed. The days were still long enough to play outside after supper, and the morning air tasted sharp and sweet—made me glad to be alive.

It didn't matter that they didn't want me. When I heard that Chuckie and Baby Grace were gone, I felt old and dead inside. Just like Mama must have felt when Krista died. It only mattered that I didn't get to say good-by.

* * *

Sister Veronica let me cry awhile before she sent me to help with supper. "It's better to keep busy, child. Things will work out, you'll see."

I found the scissors in the back of the utility cupboard next to the cook stove. I was looking for the cutter to peel potatoes for supper. We had potatoes almost every night at St. Stephen's. Sometimes Cook traded potatoes to a man who raised rabbits. Then we had rabbit stew and dumplings for a while.

Cook used those scissors to cut up the rabbits. I used them to cut off my hair.

"Loose hair is a sign of vanity," Sister Veronica had said, so I had kept mine braided and coiled on top of my head. When I helped in the kitchen, I had to wear a piece of netting over it.

Right after I found the scissors and the potato peeler on the same shelf, Sister Anne came running to fetch Cook.

"There's a mouse in the pantry!" she screeched.

Cook grabbed a hunk of the *Examiner,* rolled it into a big tube, and took off running. Sister Anne lifted her skirts and ran after her. I could hear them banging and knocking things all over the pantry.

I thought how they'd never catch the mouse that way. It was best to find his hole and plug it up with steel wool. Mama always said, "A mouse won't chew through steel wool. He'll just give up and go back outside where he belongs."

I guess it was wicked not to tell them that, to let them go ahead and wreck the pantry. Even worse to take the netting off my hair, uncoil the braid and cut right through the thickest part.

I felt sorry afterward.

Cook didn't even notice, but Sister Anne knew right away. "Oh, dear Lord," she made the sign and put both hands over her mouth. "Cissy Marie, what have you done?"

I couldn't think what to say. The braid was in my hand and my hair was sticking out all over my head. It felt soft at the top and prickly at the ends, and I thought, *I'm glad there aren't any mirrors at St. Stephen's.*

They didn't lock me in my room or make me stand against the wall at supper. Sister Anne took the braid and handed me the whisk broom. "Please clean the hair off the floor, Cissy," she said and hurried off.

Everyone pretended there was nothing different. I never found out if they caught the mouse.

Chapter
Twenty-one

I **behaved myself** at St. Stephen's, even though I was lonely.
They let me tend the little ones. That helped some, except it
reminded me of how much I missed Chuckie and Krista.

For instance, one day I was changing Baby Jacob's diaper.
His mama died when he was born and his papa didn't have a
job, so he brought the baby to St. Stephen's and asked would
they please take him? I only know 'cause I was in Sister Veronica's office when they brought the baby in. She had called me
in to give me duties for the week when Baby Jacob's papa came
in with the social lady and gave the baby over.

"Go on about your chores, girl," Sister said and pushed me
out the door. "You don't need to snoop in other people's business!"

I went on out and straightened up the day room like she said,
but next day Sister asked would I like to help with Baby Jacob
for a while? "Sister Maude is down with pleurisy this morning
and can't tend to the nursery."

I said yes, even though changing diapers and feeding bottles
wasn't what I liked best. But I knew what to do because of
Baby Grace, and it sure beat scrubbing floors and peeling onions in the kitchen.

Like I said, I was changing Baby Jacob's diaper when Sister Veronica walked in and said, "Come with me, Cissy Marie." I wondered what I'd done wrong, but before I could ask, Sister added, "We've found a place for you. Right here in Pasadena."

She took me to her office. A lady about Mama's age sat stiff and proper in the straight-backed chair in front of Sister Veronica's desk. She had on a black crepe dress, and I'd have thought she was in mourning except for the stiff white collar that looked about to strangle her. It occurred to me maybe that was why her face was so red and her eyes bulged out like she'd swallowed a peppercorn. It also occurred to me it'd be rude to ask.

A man stood behind the chair twisting the ribbon on his gray felt hat and rubbing his fat mustaches with polished pink fingers. They weren't really polished, of course. His hands were just pink and flabby, soft as Baby Jacob's bottom. I didn't know then that he buffed the nails to shining every morning. Sister gave me a swat for staring.

"Stand up, Cissy, and behave. This is Mr. and Mrs. Wilks. They've asked for a girl to help keep house and cook. You'll have your room and board, and go to Rosewood Public School."

"She don't look very strong, Ezra." Mrs. Wilks sounded for all the world like Judy Thomas when she whined!

"I'm not sure she'll do. My back's not good, you know," she complained to Sister Veronica.

"I'm sure," Sister nodded with proper sympathy. "But Cissy is strong as a horse. Helped her mama all the time, poor soul."

I wasn't sure I liked being compared to a horse, and my mama's soul was never poor. Her mind may have wandered some but her soul was just fine, thank you very much. Of course, I never said that out loud, but I thought it just the same. And meant it.

Mrs. Wilks still looked doubtful as she looked me up and

down over the top of her gold-rimmed glasses. They sat uneasy on the tip of her nose and made me want to reach right out and push them back where they belonged. But they never fell off, no matter how she shook her head or how far she bent over to pick up a stick to switch me with. Not in front of Sister Veronica, of course, but later, when I didn't do things to her liking.

I knew right off it wasn't going to be any fun. My first day with the Wilkses was Saturday. We had chicken stewed with onions in a pot for dinner. They ate in the dining room and I ate in the kitchen. "In your rightful place," Mrs. Wilks said.

I was to do the dishes and bring Mr. Wilks a piece of cake and a cup of coffee when I was through.

While I dried the plates, I looked out the window at the yard. It was a fancy yard, with soft, green grass I knew would tickle my toes if I walked on it barefoot. A real rose garden too.

"Just like in a picture book, hey little girl?" Mr. Wilks came up behind me and leaned over to look out the window too. "If you're a good girl, I'll show you the garden tomorrow," he said and rubbed his fat pink fingers across my cheek.

Just then Mrs. Wilks walked in and grabbed the dish away from me. "Where's Mr. Wilks's cake and coffee?" she howled. Her nostrils flared, then pinched together when she breathed, and her eyes popped even farther from her forehead.

Mr. Wilks smoothed his mustache and went back to the dining room.

"You're here to work, not lollygag around," Mrs. Wilks yelled, grabbing a yardstick from behind the door.

Smack! She got me good across the back of both legs before I even saw it coming. "You mind your business and don't sass me." Another smack. "I don't have time to coddle a crybaby."

Mr. Wilks ate his cake and drank his coffee and wiped off his mustache with a linen hankie. He pretended not to notice my red legs and drippy eyes. His smile gave me the willies.

I was supposed to go to Rosewood School Monday through Friday, just like regular, but I made it only once or twice a week. Got in trouble for it too. My teacher didn't believe me when I told her I had to stay home and do my work or get a licking.

She believed Mrs. Wilks, though. Mrs. Wilks said how I was slow and lazy and missed the bus on school mornings because I dawdled around in bed. And how was she supposed to bring me in when Mr. Wilks had already gone to work and her with a bad back and all?

Mrs. First made me stay after school on the days I went to make up all the work I missed. But that just put me behind on chores at home, and Mrs. Wilks would get her switch and lock me in the broom closet during dinner.

We had cornmeal mush with bread and butter every morning. I wasn't to ever touch the milk. "It comes too dear," whined Mrs. Wilks. "I keep it just for Mister's coffee. And leave the cake alone. You'll not get sugar till you earn your keep."

I never got a piece of cake.

They took me back to St. Stephen's after four whole weeks. "She's lazy," Mrs. Wilks said to Sister Veronica. "She never finishes her chores and don't tend to her lessons right. I'll be switched if I can do a thing with her."

Sister shook her head, clucked her tongue, and sent me to the chapel to "contemplate my sins."

I liked the chapel. It was quiet in there and dark, except for little white candles set in niches in the walls. I knelt down by the altar to talk to God.

Anne tiptoed in for a minute. I saw her from the corner of my eye and thought how I might be in trouble for sitting so near the altar cloth. The cloth was hand-embroidered linen and, according to Anne, "the dickens to keep clean." But Anne just smiled and left me to my prayers.

I wasn't asking for forgiveness like Sister Veronica said I

should. Instead, I told God I never did a thing to be ashamed of at the Wilkses' and I was glad they brought me back.

I really wished he'd blast them both with lightning and send them to the devil so they couldn't torment any other children. Then I realized how wicked that thought was. I had to ask forgiveness for real and was almost late for supper.

Chapter
Twenty-two

My next position was better. Mrs. Simpson liked me. She even fixed my hair so it would look presentable. She combed it out and trimmed it straight in a dutch-boy style. "It doesn't look half bad, Cissy," she insisted. "In fact, I think it suits you."

She told me how they'd never had a girl. "And we only had one child," she sighed. Then she got a faraway look in her eyes, like Mama when she talked to Papa or Krista after they were gone.

"Did he die?"

I didn't mean to blurt it out like that. Mama would say I wasn't thinking and she'd be right. But Mrs. Simpson only nodded when I apologized. "It's all right, Cissy," she whispered. "He passed on some time ago."

Then she smiled, a real smile that reached her eyes. "I know," she said, "let's go bake a cake. We'll surprise Mr. Simpson when he comes home from work."

Mrs. Simpson saw I got to school and showed me how to do the chores "fast and efficient," so I'd have time to study and maybe even read a book. The Simpsons had a room just filled with books! Fat ones, skinny ones, brown and black and green ones. Some so old the yellow paper would crumple if I touched them so I must never pick them up or turn a page.

If I got my dusting done, and studies too, I could choose one from the second shelf to read. I curled up every evening for a week with *The Adventures of Huckleberry Finn* by a man named Mark Twain. I thought, *What a handsome name,* and really got to like Huck even if he was sort of a naughty boy who smoked and cursed and took blood oaths. But not Huck's pap. No, I never did like him.

Mr. Simpson was nice. He'd come in after supper and ask if I wanted to play a game of chess or Chinese checkers. Then he put Benny Goodman on the phonograph and taught me how to do the fox trot and the swing. The social lady came one day for a surprise visit and that was the end of that.

She told Mrs. Simpson, "The very idea of that man dancing with this child turns my blood cold. It's the devil's business, that's what." And she dragged me off the next day—back to the orphanage.

Sister shook her head and clucked her tongue again. The social lady said how I should know better, and how they ought to find a place to keep me out of mischief, and didn't I have any kin to come and take me home?

Sister Veronica put me to bed without any supper. I was still the only one my age, so I slept in a closet next to her office by the entrance hall.

I lay quiet and thought how I should just pack up my sweater and my extra dress and walk right out the door. I could find Chuckie and take him to Mississippi and we could find a log cabin, and build a raft, and live on fish and berries, and we could be together till he grew up.

The closet door squeaked open real slow. It gave me a fright until I saw Sister Veronica standing with a tray, looking up and down the hall, like Jake's little brother Tim when he didn't want to get caught stealing ginger snaps.

Sister pulled the light chain, then kicked the door shut with her foot and handed me the tray. That chicken soup and soda crackers tasted like milk and honey from the Bible!

Sister sat down on the bed and watched me eat. When I slurped up the last spoonful, she set the tray down by the door and tucked the blankets underneath my chin.

"Cissy," she said so soft even a mouse couldn't hear, "I know you're a good girl, I feel it right here." She put her hand atop her bosom, right over her heart. "I know all this is hard for you, losing your family and all. Think hard now, child. Isn't there any other kin who might keep you?"

"No, Ma'am," I shook my head. Mama used to have a brother, but they never talked about him much. Papa said, "He's dead to us," but wouldn't tell me how he died. "Grandma Eva was the only other family we had, and she passed on when I was nine."

"Eva who, Cissy?" She looked real interested in Mama's mother. "What was your Grandma Eva's last name?"

I didn't know, just couldn't remember. We always called her Grandma Eva, never anything else. Even Mama and Papa called her that—at least as long as I was old enough to know.

"Well, never mind." Sister Veronica picked up the tray and pulled the light chain. "Someone will want you, child," she said into the darkness. "The good Lord knows you need a home."

Next day I went to stay on River Road in a little town called Bear Bluff, in the mountains above San Bernardino.

* * *

Mrs. Stout had six children and no husband. She relied on orphan girls that she could feed and clothe in exchange for help around the house. I explained I wasn't any orphan. My mama and papa were still alive, just couldn't care for me is all. She said that made no never mind. I was a big girl and had experience tending young'uns and that was all she needed to know.

"I haven't had a minute to myself in ten years or more," she yawned, and reached out a heavy freckled hand to swat a dirty rubber band out of her two-year-old's mouth. "Spit that out, Bobby Joe, or you'll choke to death before you can turn three!"

I didn't know it then, but right about the time I began to clean and cook and scrub little children for fat old Mrs. Stout, the social lady found out Grandma Eva's last name and started looking for lost kinfolk who could take me home.

Chapter
Twenty-three

I hadn't been at Mrs. Stout's two days when Betty Lynn told me exactly how it was.

"I'm ten," she snarled from her side of our double bed. "You're only three years older and I don't have to do what you say!"

Betty Lynn was a redhead. All six Stouts were redheads, seven if you counted Mrs. Stout, but hers had faded to a brassy yellow. And all their names began with *B*.

Betty Lynn was two inches taller and twenty pounds heavier than me, and I knew I couldn't make her mind unless she wanted to. I also knew she was out to make my life miserable, so I said, "If you don't mind me, I'll skin you alive and nail your hide to the wall!"

That wasn't a very Christian thing to say, but I'd read it in one of Mr. Simpson's books and thought it sounded mean enough to scare her.

It didn't.

The very next day we were walking down the hill to catch the school bus. I was trying to hold onto Billy Ray and wipe Bessy Ann's nose with my hankie, when Betty Lynn picked up a pine twig and flung mud all over the front of my clean dress.

Chapter Twenty-three

"Ooops! Sorry," she said, all innocent and sweet as sugar candy.

I knew she'd done it on purpose, and she knew I knew it too. But there was nothing I could do about it 'cause I had to take the little ones to school or catch trouble from Mrs. Stout. So I sat all day in a new eighth-grade class and listened to giggles from the girls and snorts from the boys and got a lecture on "cleanliness is next to godliness" from my teacher.

I tried to get Betty Lynn to like me. I called a truce and treated her "with the respect due the oldest child," like she asked me to, but it didn't make any difference.

She followed me around the house, and when I straightened up the bookshelf, she would knock the books all kittywampus on the floor. When I scrubbed the kitchen counter, she'd make herself a peanut-butter sandwich and leave another mess for me to clean. Betty Lynn made my life a misery for weeks. Then she put her own goose in the pot and turned it on to boil.

Mrs. Stout said would I please make a batch of fudge, as she had company coming from down the mountain. "A friend I haven't seen in a coon's age," she said and took a swipe at Baby Bubba's bottom as he squatted on the floor instead of telling someone "potty."

I cleaned up Baby Bubba and mopped the red linoleum, then put him and Bobby Joe down for their naps. Billy Ray and Bessy Ann were playing house with the cushions from the sofa. Really, she was playing house and he was playing fort, but it didn't bother either one of them. Becky Sue was drawing pictures at the kitchen table with the new paper pad and pencil she got for her eight-year birthday. That's how come she knew what happened to the fudge.

I went fishing in the cupboard for a pan to mix the milk and butter when I saw Betty Lynn through the kitchen window. She was leaning on the fencepost, still in her school dress, showing off a bright green piece of bubble glass to Margie Thompson, who lived across the road.

I thought how I should tell her to change her dress, but I knew she wouldn't listen, so I let it be. Her mama left to get the mail from the post box half a mile away. The first time I saw that I asked why didn't she send Betty Lynn or one of the others, but she said, "No. I like to get the mail myself. Besides, the exercise is good for my aching bones." I came to believe her only aching bone was the headache she got from all those young'uns chattering and fussing and wanting things all at once.

Anyway, she walked right by Betty Lynn and didn't say hoot about the dress, so why should I turn Betty Lynn's attention on me when her mama didn't care? And with Betty Lynn otherwise occupied, it was a good time for me to make the fudge.

I melted up the butter and poured in the milk, but before I could add the sugar and the chocolate and start the stirring that always seemed to take forever, Billy Ray shot Bessy Ann's baby doll with his rubber-band gun and I had to save him from a scalping. She had him by the hair roots and would have yanked them out all at once if I hadn't pried her off and showed her Dolly wasn't hurt.

"She needs a nap, that's all," I told Bessy Ann as I dug handfuls of Billy Ray's hair from between her fingers and put the doll in her arms. "She'll be fine when she wakes up."

Billy Ray quit screaming when I offered to get the iodine for his sore head. He agreed to take the wooden gun outside and leave Bessy Ann to sing her doll-child to sleep.

For a minute, I could almost see Chuckie and Krista playing on the rose garden rug in the living room on York Street. But I didn't have time to get all teary eyed. I smelled sugar scorching in the kitchen. Funny. I thought I'd turned the fire off when I left the room.

Sure enough, there stood Betty Lynn, grinning from ear to ear, stirring sugar into the pan. She'd already dumped in the chocolate, and she wasn't stirring fast enough. I snatched the pan off the burner and left her holding the handle of her mama's blue-enamel baking spoon. I should have known there was trouble when she smiled wide and handed me the spoon like I'd done her a favor taking over.

Becky Sue bent almost double over her paper pad. I thought how she didn't want me to see her picture and maybe she was drawing a surprise. I wondered if it was for me.

The fudge set up stiff and pretty. All swirly dips and circles on the top. When it was cool enough, I cut it into matching squares and put it on the fancy cut-glass cake plate Mrs. Stout saved for company best.

The children were excited all through dinner. Billy Ray even ate his broccoli, but he kept one eye glued on that plate of fudge. Mrs. Stout's friend, Emma, showed up at half past seven. A half hour later than expected. It was near impossible to keep the little ones clean that long, and Bessy Ann got a swat for trying to sneak a piece of fudge off the plate.

Emma was the biggest woman I've ever seen before or since. She had to squeeze through the front door sideways, and she took up two whole cushions on the couch. Her stockings scrunched down around the ankles and her dirty feet spilled out over the tops of her shoes. They were the slip-on kind, at least a size too small, but Miss Emma said it didn't matter, seeing how she couldn't see them anyway, ha ha, and please pass the fudge.

Billy Ray and Bessy Ann held their breath. I could see them draw it in and wait, wondering if Miss Emma would eat the whole plate by herself. Becky Sue sort of backed off into the corner by the bookshelf and Betty Lynn just stood there grinning to beat the band.

I knew then that something was up and tried to figure what it was so I could maybe head it off before it happened. But I didn't think fast enough.

Miss Emma shoved two pieces in her mouth at once, closed her eyes and smacked her lips, and swiped at a stream of chocolate that dripped down her pudgy chin. Next thing I knew she was coughing and choking and grabbing at her neck, spitting fudge all over herself and the sofa.

Mrs. Stout wrung her hands and screamed, "Oh dear, oh dear, Miss Emma's dying, whatever will we do?"

About that time, Betty Lynn turned white. I guess she thought maybe Miss Emma really would die. Anyway, she started bawling and pointing in my direction. "It's soap," she wailed. "It's soap. Cissy put soap flakes in the fudge. She's killed Miss Emma, Mama, Cissy's killed Miss Emma."

Things happened fast after that. Faster than lightning at a July picnic. I grabbed the plate of fudge away from Bessy Ann and pried a good-size piece out of Baby Bubba's mouth. Miss Emma caught her breath and held her stomach while Mrs. Stout tried to hoist her from the sofa. Bobby Joe got scared and threw up all over Billy Ray, and the whole passel of them set up a hullabaloo you could hear from here to Tuesday.

When Miss Emma finally made it out the door and down the hill, Mrs. Stout came back in from the driveway breathing fire. I do believe you could have fried a chicken on her forehead. Her face was red enough to match her hair before it faded brassy yellow. Someone was going to get a whipping sure.

Poor Becky Sue. She'd scooted back behind the bookshelf as far as she could go, but it wasn't far enough to hide her. I know she must have thought as how she would get it either way the turkey flew. She was the one hiding and Mrs. Stout knew good and well I hadn't done it like Betty Lynn said. Becky Sue had to tell—on Betty Lynn, I mean.

Mrs. Stout dragged Betty Lynn out to the garage. I put the little ones in their beds and they stayed first time, even Bobby Joe. Becky Sue tried to help clean up the mess, but her hands shook so I told her never mind. She knew she was in trouble too—for not telling sooner how Betty Lynn snuck in the kitchen and shaved flakes of Ivory Soap with the paring knife into the pan of fudge. Betty Lynn had threatened to burn her paper pad and pencil if she told.

Betty Lynn had to eat standing up for a week, and if I so much as bumped her in our bed she set up a howl. Becky Sue needn't have worried about her paper pad. Betty Lynn's mama watched her like a hawk and told her what would happen if Becky Sue's pad ever disappeared.

Chapter
Twenty-four

I don't know if Betty Lynn ever did get even. Two weeks after the trouble with the fudge, the social lady came to call.

I thought, *Oh no, not the orphanage again!* 'Cause even though I worked real hard and Betty Lynn made so much trouble and there was never any milk and hardly enough food, I'd gotten to like the little ones. Mrs. Stout treated me almost like a grown-up and saw to it that I got to school and had a dress to wear.

But the social lady said I would only be at the orphanage a day or so. "Just until they sign the papers, Cissy Marie. Your mama has a brother named Edward," she said, smiling to beat the band, "and he's agreed to take you sight unseen. What do you say to that?"

I didn't have a thing to say. I was struck as dumb as Zechariah when he disbelieved the Lord.

I could sure think, though. I thought how there was some mistake. Mama's brother died before I was born. We only had Grandma Eva, who had passed on three years ago. At least Mama never spoke of anyone, and surely Papa would have said something when Mama came down sick and me and Chuckie and Baby Grace had to go to other homes.

'Course, I knew what would happen sure as I was born. Mama's brother-by-mistake would take one look at me and say, "That's not my kin!" and send me back to the orphanage faster than greased lightning. I'd lose my place with Mrs. Stout— she'd sure need other help in the meantime—and maybe have to go to someone like the Wilkses. Maybe worse!

I started bawling; I couldn't help it. The thought of starting all over again was more than I could stand. I blubbered all over the social lady and bawled all over Mrs. Stout. They must have thought I was crying for joy, because they laughed and hugged me hard, and said to kiss the little ones good-by and they would miss me and have a good new life.

Then I met Uncle Edward and Aunt Rosie and heard how they'd been trying to find me since the day Uncle Edward saw in the paper about Papa being in prison and accused of murder.

By the time they signed the papers and took me home, it was three days to Christmas. That was when I cried for joy. Uncle Edward and Aunt Rosie were the best presents I ever had.

* * *

I sure admired cousin Mary Margaret, but I don't think she liked me much at first.

When Uncle Edward and Aunt Rosie brought me home, Mary Margaret was sitting on the sofa, next to my other new-found cousin, Billy, wearing her periwinkle-blue dress. Her hair was done up in finger curls like always, the sides pulled back and fastened with a blue velvet ribbon. Little bits of hair fell down like corkscrews right along her cheeks. She calls them wisps. "All the style, you know," she says whenever she wants to put on airs. But then she's two years older than me and really educated about beauty and fashion and all.

I didn't know that then, of course. She glared at me, brown eyes alive with mischief, cheeks colored with her mother's rouge, and I thought, *Oh no! Another Betty Lynn!* I felt like I'd jumped into the ocean with a shark and was about to get swallowed whole!

Billy made me feel some better. He jumped right up and started asking questions, like: Did I like chicken, 'cause we were having it for supper, and did I bring him something, and did I know anything about baseball or making apple pie?

Uncle Edward told him, "Hush, go wash your hands for dinner," and pointed him toward the hall.

It didn't take all that long to get to know Aunt Rosie, Uncle Edward, Mary Margaret and Billy. They were nice and treated me like family, even if I was the long-lost kind.

* * *

On Christmas day, after breakfast and presents, Uncle Edward took me for a walk. I wore the new white sweater they'd given me that morning, but the sun was sparkling off the red-tile roofs and we hadn't got two blocks before I had to take it off.

Uncle Edward cleared his throat and explained why it had taken so long for them to find me. He told how he and Mama had a fight when she wanted to marry Papa.

"She was much too young," Uncle Edward said. "We thought Charles wasn't good enough to have her, was too fond of the bottle. But he loved your mama, and your mama loved him, and they were dead set to marry!" Uncle Edward told them not to call on him for help, and he didn't even stay for the wedding.

He didn't know, till later, that I'd been born.

So I told him how my parents moved to Pike, Nevada, and Papa got the job at the bank and stopped his drinking during Prohibition, and went to church with us, and later came to Jesus two days after I did at the big tent meeting just outside of town.

I remembered that like yesterday. Mama cried for a week and hugged us both every time we turned around and told everyone in town about it. She was that proud and happy!

Uncle Edward said he tried to find us. He and Aunt Rosie had found Jesus too, and they wanted to make amends with Mama and Papa. But no one knew where we'd gone off to except for Grandma Eva, and Papa had forbidden her to tell.

Uncle Edward stayed quiet for a while and I thought something was wrong. Maybe they were having second thoughts and didn't want me to stay. My stomach started doing flips. But before I could be sick, Uncle Edward put his arm around my shoulder.

"Cissy, you've been through a lot this last year or so, and I think you're old enough to know the truth."

At St. Stephen's I'd learned to be quiet when a grownup was talking, so I just watched my shoes step across the cracks in the sidewalk and waited for Uncle Edward to go on.

"Your mother is sick, Cissy. She can't think straight all the time, so she's in a hospital where they can take care of her."

I knew that was true. Mama hadn't been herself for months.

"Will she get better?" I wondered.

"I hope so, sweetheart. But I don't think it will be right away."

"What about Papa?"

Uncle Edward didn't seem to mind my questions. He just hugged my shoulders tighter. "Your father is in prison, Cissy, and he might be there for a long time. Someone said he killed a man named Lou Berdowski. Your father denies it, but murder is a serious charge."

That made me mad. If Papa said he didn't do it, I believed him. Uncle Edward wouldn't tell who said it, but I'd have bet my allowance for a year it was Susi Cummings's stinking brother Roy!

"You have to be brave," Uncle Edward told me as we came around the block toward home. "Be brave and trust in God to see you through."

Uncle Edward said he would find Chuckie and Grace and bring them home. But later, when he tried, no one would tell where they were. The social lady said how it was best for Chuckie to stay with his new family.

"He's already made a hard adjustment," she said. "It would be too traumatic to move the boy again." Uncle Edward got a lawyer, but the law agreed with the social lady and that was that.

I hope Chuckie remembers what I told him about heaven.

Chapter
Twenty-five

Mary Margaret told me later that she liked me fine when she found I wasn't a snob and could have fun with her just like a friend. That was after the day we made taffy in Aunt Rosie's kitchen and made a mess and got in trouble.

Billy started it. "I'm bored," he whined, like he'd whined every afternoon of Easter break. It hadn't rained almost all year in San Bernardino. But now that school was out for a week, it decided to pour, keeping us stuck indoors. Hadn't stopped since it started on Sunday night—and this was Thursday!

"I know," said Mary Margaret, "let's make taffy. Mama's got the recipe around here somewhere."

"Yippee! What flavor?" Billy started jerking open kitchen drawers.

"Be still," Mary Margaret hissed, and gave him a swat to show she was in charge. "Look in that cupboard, Cissy, and see what Mama has." Mary Margaret pointed to the shelves above the sink where Aunt Rosie kept the baking things. "I'll get out the sugar and the mixing bowl. Billy, get the butter from the ice box."

"Here's peppermint and lemon, and licorice too," I said, lifting down the tiny bottles like they were fancy crystal. "Are you sure you know how to make taffy?" I remembered the fudge at Mrs. Stout's and I didn't want that kind of trouble at Aunt Rosie's.

"Of course I do." Mary Margaret stuck her chest out in a huff. "I've made it lots of times."

"Have not," said Billy real low, but Mary Margaret heard and glared him down.

"Maybe not all by myself," she huffed some more, "but I helped Mama lots of times. It's easy." She snatched the butter out of Billy's hand and dug the heavy saucepan from the stove drawer.

Like I said, I admired Mary Margaret. She measured out the sugar and molasses and stirred it like she'd been doing it for real all her life. I handed her vinegar and soda, while Billy hopped back and forth from foot to foot, hollering, "I get to help pull it! I get to help you pull!"

Mary Margaret ignored him. She stirred in the butter and soda, then told me to grease the counter.

"What?" I said. I thought I'd heard her wrong. "Don't you want the cookie sheet?"

"Why bother? Anyway, the counter is bigger. Just rub some butter on it, so I can turn this out."

She looked at me impatiently, so I rubbed some butter on the counter. She dumped the sticky blob of candy in the middle and spread it with the back of the mixing spoon.

Soon as it was cool enough to handle, Mary Margaret said it was time to pull. But there were three of us, and taking turns didn't sound like too much fun. That's when Billy got the idea to use the handles on the cupboard doors.

I don't know why Mary Margaret and I didn't try to stop him. I guess we were too busy having a good time to think past pulling and tasting that taffy.

We greased our hands up good and pulled and braided, licking off our fingers in between each rope. We didn't even notice how messy we'd got the kitchen till Mary Margaret went to get the paper scissors off the service porch so we could cut the candy into hunks. She turned back into the kitchen and I heard her suck in air like someone hit her in the stomach.

"Oh, my!" she said, sounding for all the world like Aunt Rosie when she got a bad surprise.

"Oh, no!"

I looked over my shoulder and there was Uncle Edward, standing in the doorway, his chin down to his knees, looking like someone had just hollered *Fire!*

I thought we were dead for sure!

It took me two days to believe what Uncle Edward did just then. He shook his head and doubled over laughing till he had to hold his sides. Then he helped us cut the candy into bite-size pieces and set about to help clean up the mess.

By the time Aunt Rosie got home from choir practice, her kitchen sparkled like a shiny dime and the taffy sat all cool and golden on a platter on the kitchen table.

"I've never tasted anything so good," she said and took a second piece.

Uncle Edward just looked at her and smiled.

Chapter
Twenty-six

Jake showed up in June.

I didn't realize how much I'd missed him until the doorbell rang and there he was, standing on the porch, a paper box down by his feet, grinning from ear to ear.

I couldn't believe it! I flung my arms around his neck and hugged him tight. Soon as I did, I could feel my face get hot, so I pushed away. But Jake wouldn't let go. He hugged me even tighter, and I could feel his breath all warm and ticklish on my neck. Then his lips brushed against my cheek and he kissed me on the mouth.

I kissed him back. I knew I shouldn't, but I couldn't help it. I felt like I'd had two swigs of Papa's whiskey, like Alice falling down the rabbit hole for real.

"Ciss-ssy Summers-ss!"

The snake hissed at me from behind the hawthorn hedge. By the time Jake heard and let me go, I could see that the snake had blonde hair curving 'round her cheeks and brown eyes big as Christmas balls. Mary Margaret's mouth was open so wide I could see down to her tonsils.

Jake straightened up his shirt and tie, breathing like he'd run all the way from York Street. He turned and bowed to Mary

Margaret like she was the queen of England and him a duke.

Mary Margaret shut her mouth, and I'll be switched if she didn't curtsy back! I introduced them proper, and we all went in the kitchen for molasses cookies and lemonade.

Jake said he found out where I was when the social worker came back to ask his mama some questions. She wouldn't tell him, of course, but she told his mama about Uncle Edward and Aunt Rosie. "Wasn't it a wonderful Christian thing to do? To take in a child, sight unseen, even if it was long-lost kin?"

Jake just waited till she left, then asked his mama what was my uncle's last name and where'd he live. His mama asked, "What are you up to?" but told him anyway. From there on it was easy. He waited till he'd worked two weeks at Mr. Gimble's drugstore, then took the streetcar to the railroad yard in Los Angeles and hopped a freight to San Bernardino.

"I'll go back the same way," he said. "It only took two hours. I can come once a month if the weather holds." He looked at me and winked, bold as you please.

Mary Margaret's mouth opened again, but she shut it quick when Uncle Edward and Aunt Rosie came through the kitchen door carrying two bags of groceries and the box Jake had brought. We must have left it on the porch.

Jake jumped up to help without being asked and handed me the box. "Some things I thought you'd like to have," he said and looked away.

It didn't take a genius to know what was in there. You could hear the growls and yowls six blocks away. I guess Tarzan was tired of being cooped up, 'cause the minute I opened the lid, he took a flying leap over my shoulder, landed on Aunt Rosie's just-waxed linoleum and slid—slick as you please—right into the broom-closet door. He shook himself off, then looked around indignant-like and set to washing his paws like he'd lived there all his life.

Billy had come in behind Aunt Rosie. "Hey, wow! A cat!" he hollered, and ran to pick him up.

Tarzan let himself be lifted to Billy's shoulder. He purred as loud as he yowled, and I looked at Aunt Rosie to see if she was going to let me keep him. She smiled, and Uncle Edward said, "Looks like we've got a cat."

The only one who didn't smile was Mary Margaret. "Why would anybody want a cat?" She screwed her lip into a snarl, wrinkled up her nose like she'd just ate a Brussels sprout, and plucked a short gray hair off the sleeve of her white sweater.

I reached back in the box and found Cecilia. Jake had wrapped her, good as new, in a piece of an old coffee sack.

I looked at Jake. He shoved both hands down in the pockets of his jeans and shrugged his shoulders. "I thought you'd want it," was all he said.

I nodded yes, 'cause I couldn't talk just then. No one else said anything either. Even Tarzan hushed his rumble and settled to sleep against Billy's flannel shirt.

The whole thing ended with Aunt Rosie calling Jake's mother, and Jake staying to dinner, and Uncle Edward driving him home afterward.

"He seems like a nice boy," Aunt Rosie said to Uncle Edward when he got back.

Uncle Edward looked at her and sighed. "He is, Rosie. A very nice young man."

They smiled at me and went into their room.

* * *

"Well," said Mary Margaret after she marched into the room and shut the door, "looks like you've got a beau." Her face looked flushed and her eyes were glassy bright. I thought maybe she had a fever and I should go get Aunt Rosie, but Mary Margaret pushed me back onto the bed. "Tell!" she squealed, then looked around like maybe someone else was in the room.

"Tell what?" I asked. "What's a beau?"

"A boyfriend—Jake, you ninny." She curled up beside me on the bed. "Why didn't you tell me about him? He's a prize. A real ring-tailed snorter."

"Mary Margaret! You know Aunt Rosie told you not to talk like that."

I knew she meant how Jake had kissed me, and I didn't want to talk about it. Not right then. I hadn't even had time to sort it out myself. Was Jake my boyfriend? We'd always been just friends before. Good friends, like blood brothers in the Tom Mix movie we saw the last time Jake took Krista and me to the Saturday show. Tom Mix and his wonder horse Tony fighting the battle for good over evil.

I can still see Chuckie standing in the living room with his cowboy gun and holster and the hat Papa bought him for a dollar twenty-five at Kress's. He would give the Straight Shooter's salute, puff out his chest and recite the entire Ralston Straight Shooter Pledge of Allegiance he'd memorized from the back of the cereal box.

That was a long time ago.

"There's nothing to tell, Mary Margaret. Anyway, you knew about Jake. He lived next door to me on York Street, remember?"

Mary Margaret hurumphed and looked offended. "All right, Cissy Marie Summers, you don't have to tell me a thing. Someday you'll come crying for my advice, and maybe I'll help you and maybe I won't."

I expected her to stick out her tongue like Judy Thomas always did whenever we had a fight. The picture made me want to laugh; my fifteen-year-old cousin with Judy Thomas's nine-year-old face.

Instead, Mary Margaret marched into the hall, and I heard the bathroom door slam.

She didn't give up, though. Uncle Edward said Mary Margaret could be tenacious when she had a bee in her bonnet. I didn't know what *tenacious* meant, but she sure could be stubborn. Worse than Jeremy Mason's old mule, Isabel.

The next day, I was playing catch with Billy and his dog, Colby, in the backyard. Billy was trying to teach me how to play baseball, but it wasn't easy to catch a ball coming right at my face. I wanted to duck and run every time he threw it to me. "Stand up straight," he hollered when I missed. "Keep your hands up and your eye on the ball!"

We had played for almost an hour and I had caught a few, which was a good thing because old Colby was huffing and puffing from having to retrieve the ball. He slunk over to his dish, slurped down about a gallon of water, and crawled under the hydrangea for a nap.

I'd just caught my third ball in a row when Mary Margaret stuck her head out of the upstairs window. "Cissy," she called sweet as syrup, "would you come up here a minute please? I have a surprise for you."

I threw the baseball back to Billy. It curved wide, hit the eucalyptus tree, bounced back toward the house and rolled to a stop in front of Colby's nose. Colby opened one eye, sighed, and went right back to sleep. Billy slapped his forehead and rolled his eyes. "Tomorrow we'll work on your throwing," he promised.

I told him sure, even though I'd rather sit in the shade with a good book and a glass of Aunt Rosie's lemonade. Billy had lots of friends, but they were all older than him and knew how to play baseball just fine. "It makes him feel important to have someone to teach," Aunt Rosie had said. So I made like I really wanted to learn, even when I found out how hard it was.

Mary Margaret shook her head when she saw my dirty hands and scabbed-up knees. "How disgusting," she clucked. "You need to take more interest in your appearance, Cissy, now that you've got a beau and all. If Jake saw you like that, he'd take the first freight car back home."

It was on the tip of my tongue to say, "He would not," and "Jake's seen me like this plenty of times," when I looked in the mirror on the wall between our beds. I guess I was a sight. My hair had grown some since I'd come to live at Uncle Edward's, and now it was all matted and wet. I had a smudge of dirt across my cheek.

I looked at Mary Margaret with her done-up curls and soft green jumper with a white-collar blouse. Her skin was creamy smooth and her hands, I knew, were as soft and pink as Tarzan's belly. She creamed them every day. Sometimes twice, when it was her turn to do the dishes and they got all red and itchy from the soap. She'd run into the bathroom and grab Aunt Rosie's jar of Ponds and rub it into her hands like she was putting out a fire.

My own hands were rough, the knuckles scraped and half a yard of dirt under my fingernails.

Suddenly, I didn't want to play ball anymore, or chase Colby around the yard, or draw hopscotch squares with the girls next door.

Suddenly, I wanted to be just like Mary Margaret.

Chapter
Twenty-seven

The surprise turned out to be a makeup kit. Mary Margaret had put it together with odds and ends of Aunt Rosie's old lipstick, powder and rouge.

"The trick is," she said after I'd washed and changed into my own brown jumper and white blouse, "to use just a little, so people can hardly tell you have it on."

I knew *people* meant Aunt Rosie. Mama would have a tizzy if she saw me wearing makeup, and I couldn't see how Aunt Rosie would be any different. Mama always said, "You mustn't wear makeup before you're sixteen. You'll look like a hussy and poison your skin besides."

When Mary Margaret finally finished patting and smoothing my cheeks, she handed me a lipstick and turned me toward the mirror. The tube was almost empty.

"It's all I could find," she said with a shrug. "Here, do it like this." She dug her little finger into the tube and brought the waxy red tip to her own lips. She painted the top one, then rubbed her lips together to spread it around.

The first time I tried it, I smeared red all over my chin and had to wash and start all over again. By supper time I had it right. Mary Margaret and I went downstairs and sat at the table without saying a word.

Uncle Edward smiled, blessed the food, and got busy with his green beans. Aunt Rosie dished up Billy's plate, then passed Mary Margaret the potatoes. "My, you girls look nice tonight. Don't they, Edward?"

Uncle Edward nodded and started to say something, but Billy put his chicken leg back on the plate and interrupted. "Cissy, how come your lip's all bloodied?"

I thought how I'd like to bloody his lip, but Aunt Rosie hushed him. "Cissy's lip is fine, William. Have some more green beans."

Billy scowled and went back to his chicken leg, but somehow I didn't feel as glamorous as Mary Margaret said I looked.

After dinner Aunt Rosie put her arm around my shoulders. "You look nice, Cissy, and it's fine to practice wearing make-up around the house. But I'd rather you wait awhile before you wear lipstick and rouge anywhere else."

She sent me up to wash. Mary Margaret started to follow me, but Aunt Rosie stopped her. "I'll have a word with you, young lady," I heard her say before I shut the bathroom door.

* * *

Jake kept his promise and came back for the Fourth of July. It turned out Jake liked baseball too, and Billy was pretty miffed when Jake started giving him some pointers.

We'd all gone to the park for the afternoon and Billy and Jake had joined a pickup game on the new field.

Billy sulked for most of the game and struck out in the second and third innings. In the fourth he missed a high fly ball and the others booed him off the field. I felt sorry for him, even though he deserved it for being such a baby.

By the top of the ninth, the bases were loaded and our team was down by three. Billy must have been desperate. He took the plate once, then backed away. The pitcher yelled, "What ya waiting for, dirt clod? You ain't gonna hit nothing anyway."

Billy looked at Jake. Jake winked and gave him the thumbs-up sign, and Billy stepped up to the plate. He adjusted his stance, took two practice swings, and gave the pitcher the evil eye.

The pitcher wound up like a spring, brought his hand to his glove for a full five seconds, then reared back and flung a hard fast ball right down the pike.

They never saw it coming. Billy smacked that ball so hard it cracked the bat, whizzed right past the pitcher's left ear, sent the center fielder spinning to his knees, and sailed on over the back fence without dropping an inch.

The crowd went wild. The other three players scored and Billy's feet barely hit home plate before the rest of the team had him on their shoulders yelling and screaming and slapping his back.

They played out the inning, but the other team couldn't score. Jake caught a line drive at first, stepped on the bag, and the game was over.

We hung around awhile afterward with Jake giving Billy more pointers and Billy hanging onto every word. One of the bigger boys from the other team came over and challenged them to a game next Saturday. Billy was feeling pretty confident and promised he'd round up some players.

"Can you come, Jake?" he asked hopefully.

Jake shrugged and shook his head. "Nah, I have to work at Gimble's."

The bigger boy looked smug. "See ya Saturday," he smirked and sauntered off.

We played catch awhile. Jake said I was getting better. "Almost like one of the guys," he said and grinned. "By the time summer's over, ol' Billy here will have you playing with the rest of them."

I wasn't sure I wanted that—to play like the rest of the guys, I mean. Mary Margaret would never be caught dead playing baseball. She was over at the playground batting her eyes at Carl Strong, helping him push his little brother, Norman, on the swings.

Mary Margaret had worn a sundress to the park. A soft, white cotton with a belt and a yellow-flowered jacket. She looked feminine and sweet, "a rose among roses," as Uncle Edward would say. People noticed when she walked by and stopped their talk to nod and smile.

Jake took her arm and helped her onto the bench when we sat down at the picnic table. My stomach felt a little funny and I only ate one piece of chicken and an ear of corn. I shook my head when Aunt Rosie passed the apple pie.

"What's wrong, Cissy?" she touched my forehead all concerned. "You never turn down apple pie."

I shrugged and swiped at a tear that started sliding down my cheek. Jake was talking to Uncle Edward. Billy and Mary Margaret were fighting over the last piece of watermelon on the tray.

Aunt Rosie patted my hand. "You miss your mama, don't you, sweetheart?"

I nodded yes, because that was partly true. I didn't know why seeing Jake help Mary Margaret made my stomach twitch.

Then suddenly I did miss Mama, more than ever. I wondered how I could be surrounded by people who loved me and still feel so lonely.

Chapter
Twenty-eight

It stayed hot all through July and August. Billy taught me how to throw a fast ball, and I helped him with his spelling and arithmetic. One hour a week was all he had to do, but you'd have thought someone had stabbed him with a hot poker the way he carried on!

Mary Margaret took me to the library once a week, and by my birthday I had almost half my list of "want-to's" read. I even finished *The Good Earth,* but I had to admit some parts were hard to understand.

The Saturday after the Fourth of July, I had finished clearing the breakfast dishes and was heading out the back door with an apple and a Nancy Drew mystery. I couldn't wait to get into it, so I started turning pages right away and nearly tripped over Billy, who was hunkered over on the bottom step.

"Ow!" he hollered, and I could see he was trying not to cry.

"I'm sorry, Billy." My foot had caught him in the back, but I didn't think it was hard enough to hurt that bad. He looked like someone had up and died.

"What's wrong?"

"Nothing," he snapped. "Go read your stupid old book."

That made me mad. First off, my book wasn't stupid. Second,

since when did he have a call to talk to me like that?

"Give over, Billy." I scooted him aside and sat as close as I dared; he was in a foul mood and I didn't want to take a punch on the arm just then. "Tell."

Billy shrugged. "The game's in half an hour and we need one more player. We'll have to forfeit, and the other guys will be mad 'cause I was supposed to set up the team."

Right then I remembered the bigger kid at the park on the Fourth. How he'd baited Billy to play another game and looked so smug when he found out Jake couldn't be there.

"I'll play."

I couldn't believe I'd said it, but it was too late to take it back. Billy's eyes lit up like sparklers.

"You'll play, Cissy? You really will?" He threw his glove in the air and caught it. "Yippee!" he yelled, then frowned and sat back down on the step.

"You're not very good," he said like I wasn't even there, "and you're a girl. The guys might not like that. But hey," he smiled again and punched my arm, "you can wear my Yankee cap and play right field. Maybe they won't even notice."

I opened my mouth to tell him, "Not on your life, if you're so rude," but he was already halfway across the yard.

"Hurry up and change," he hollered over his shoulder. "Meet me at the sandlot, and don't forget what I taught ya."

I didn't forget.

The other guys looked at me like I had the measles, but Billy convinced them that without me they wouldn't get a chance to play at all. I made up my mind they'd be sorry for treating me that way.

I was nervous at first and dropped the ball twice in the first two innings, but no one scored and by the time it was my turn to bat I felt pretty good. I hit a grounder that slid right through the third baseman's legs, and I made first base without even running hard. The next batter drove the ball right through left-center field for a double, and the next one brought me home.

The game was close: three to two at the bottom of the ninth. We ended up losing on an error, but it wasn't me that did it. The teams shook hands and the bigger boy we'd seen at the park said I was a sport and could come play for them anytime.

I decided baseball was fun, even for a girl.

* * *

I had the dream for the first time around the end of August. Right after Uncle Edward took us to the county fair.

Mary Margaret had just turned sweet sixteen, and Uncle Edward wanted to do something special. "Something we'll remember as a family," he said at dinner the night before.

Billy didn't give Mary Margaret time to think. "I know," he shouted with his mouth full of mashed potatoes, "let's go to the fair!"

Uncle Edward looked surprised, Aunt Rosie said, "William, don't talk with your mouth full," and we all looked at Mary Margaret.

I thought for sure she'd glare him daggers or kick him under the table. Instead, she took the time to chew a bite of pineapple-glazed ham Aunt Rosie had cooked for her birthday dinner.

Mary Margaret did love ham. It was expensive though. We'd just had it at Easter, and Aunt Rosie had to convince Uncle Edward. "We do without the extras most of the time," she reminded him, "and I'm grateful how the Lord supplies, but we've always let the children choose their favorite meal on their birthdays." The ham was on the counter the very next day.

Anyway, Mary Margaret took her time, then looked around the table, smiled sweetly, and said, "I think it's a great idea."

Billy whooped and upset his water glass. When Aunt Rosie rushed to grab a kitchen towel, he fed his last bite of carrots to Colby, who waited patiently underneath the table.

I saw, but didn't tell. Billy did that all the time. I don't see how Aunt Rosie couldn't know, and besides, everyone was too happy then to make a fuss. Everyone but Uncle Edward. His face looked funny underneath his smile. "Well," he said, "it's settled then," and pushed back from the table.

Later, when I went in to say good night, I saw Aunt Rosie sifting through her grocery money. The box on the dresser that held Uncle Edward's pocket change was empty. I knew if we went to the fair we'd eat pancakes or dumplings for supper twice next week.

* * *

It was a long drive to Pomona, and morning was gone by the time we reached the fairgrounds. The sun-hot pavement burned my toes and I had to put on my shoes as soon as we got out of the car. I could smell the sweet, scorched smell of cotton candy from where we parked a block away.

Mary Margaret wore her sundress again. Aunt Rosie said to wear the jacket too: "You'll get a burn, young lady." But Mary Margaret left it on the back seat of the Buick. If Aunt Rosie noticed, she didn't say anything.

There must have been a thousand people there—all happy, waving flags, and rushing around. Billy scowled when Aunt Rosie said, "Hold my hand." But he did it anyway.

The noontime air hummed with music from the carousel calliope. Barkers on the midway shouted to the crowd: "Get your popcorn here! Three balls for a nickel! Pitch a penny for a prize!"

Some boys in sailor hats ran by whirling rainbow-colored pinwheels and pushed their way ahead of us in line. Uncle Edward counted out admission, then handed us three tickets each. "Choose your rides carefully now," he said.

Billy wanted to spend all his right then, but Aunt Rosie suggested we do other things first and save the rides till "after your lunch has settled."

Billy got to pet a cow and decided he could never live without a pony. A big old sow had baby pigs. They squealed and slurped and stank to high heaven.

When a nanny goat tried to eat Mary Margaret's pocketbook, she said she had "had enough of animals," so Uncle Edward finished taking Billy around the livestock pens while Aunt Rosie, Mary Margaret and I oohed and aahed over fancy stitchery and quilts.

By supper time we'd had our fill of caramel apples, popcorn and cotton candy. While Billy whirled on the swings, Mary Margaret sipped Coca Cola through a straw and batted her eyelashes at Wesley Harris, a boy she knew from school.

We saved the Ferris wheel for last.

The sun had drifted down behind the barns, and the sky had faded from blue to gray toward the mountains, but there still was a red and orange glow in the west. The wheel was lit up like a Christmas tree. We stood awhile and watched it sail around and around. When it finally stopped and it was our turn to ride, they made us sit together: Mary Margaret and me, with Billy in the middle.

The first few minutes my stomach flipped when the wheel jerked and stopped to let new people on. Billy kept kicking his feet to make our seat rock, and Mary Margaret threatened to box his ears if he didn't keep still.

Finally, the wheel spun. We soared and dipped, rose and fell, the wind whistling in our ears and ruffling our hair. I closed my eyes, breathed in deep, and rode the wheel like an eagle flying free.

Then we stopped. Our seat swung right at the very top and I felt like I could see the world. *Is this what Grandma Eva sees when she looks down from heaven?*

Lights snapped on all over the fairgrounds. People scurried

everywhere, their faces blurred, the colors of their clothing lost in a jumble of distance and light.

Directly below, a man and woman stood with their arms around each other looking up at the wheel and waving. *Was it Uncle Edward and Aunt Rosie?* I wondered. Behind them, a man shielded his eyes and looked up too. He wasn't waving though, just staring like he could see right through me.

Billy kicked his legs once more and set the car rocking. I turned my head and looked at Mary Margaret. Her face was as white as one of Aunt Rosie's new-washed sheets. I was sure she'd lose her lunch any minute. Then the wheel moved and started down. By the time we got off, Billy's feet were quiet, Mary Margaret looked some better, and the man standing behind Uncle Edward was gone.

On the ride home, Billy fell asleep against Aunt Rosie's shoulder. I must have dozed off too because the drive didn't seem to take as long as when we came.

We all went straight to bed after telling Uncle Edward, "Thank you for the lovely time."

*   *   *

The dream was all mixed up and crazy, like the patchwork on the quilt that won first prize at the fair. The places in the dream were real, but the faces were all different, and everything was sad or frightening instead of fun.

I'd dreamed the first part several times before.

I saw the man and lady standing by the car outside St. Stephen's. I saw her ring and painted nails, and her hand resting on the sleeve of his navy pin-stripe suit. But this time I could see her face, Mama's face looking up and smiling at the man. Not Papa. I tried and tried to see him, but I couldn't tell who it was.

Then the picture changed and I was at the fair again, flying round and round on the Ferris wheel. This time when the wheel stopped at the top I saw the faces clearly: Uncle Edward and Aunt Rosie looking up at us, laughing and waving.

The man standing behind them took his hand away from his eyes. Susi Cummings's brother Roy.

I felt sick to my stomach, and all at once we were on the spinner at the carnival in Pike, me and Susi Cummings and Krista, who was throwing up. Susi and I yelled and yelled until they finally stopped the ride.

I jerked awake and ran into the bathroom. Aunt Rosie came to check on me, got me a cool cloth for my face and pulled out the milk of magnesia. "Too much excitement, Cissy," she said, "and that caramel apple was much too rich for you."

I thought how my getting sick had nothing to do with the caramel apple and wondered why Roy Cummings still made me feel so afraid.

Chapter
Twenty-nine

My birthday came around fast enough. I wouldn't have spent any time wishing for it if I'd known what it would bring.

I heard a whippoorwill call from the eucalyptus tree in the yard behind my window. When I opened my eyes it was already light. Mary Margaret's bed was empty. She'd made it up proper and hung her nightgown on the hook next to the dresser. I thought I was in trouble for sure.

I could hear whooping and hollering coming from the sandlot on the corner. I just knew I'd slept past morning and they'd started the game without me. I jumped out of bed and pulled on a pair of Billy's old hand-me-down jeans and a flannel shirt. It was all I could find. I threw my pajamas under the pillow and covered the whole mess with the chenille spread. Maybe Aunt Rosie wouldn't notice until after the game.

I thought I had it made. No one was upstairs. Colby whined and licked my ankle when I tiptoed through the living room, but I hushed him with a pat on the head.

I'd have been out the front door in a flash if I hadn't got a craving for a glass of milk. I snatched Billy's old Yankee cap from the rack by the stairs and headed for the kitchen. I no sooner pushed through the door than they were all over me.

"Surprise! Surprise!" they yelled. All of them. Aunt Rosie standing at the sink. Uncle Edward folding up the morning paper.

Billy wasn't playing baseball. He sat there at the kitchen table, grinning like the Cheshire Cat, making goofy faces, and pointing to a big box on the table in front of my chair. It was beautiful. All wrapped up neat and pretty in the Sunday funnies.

Mary Margaret grabbed my arm and led me over. Boy, was I surprised. I felt like someone had gone and made it Christmas all over again.

I blushed and mumbled something like, "Sorry I overslept," and, "You shouldn't have got me anything." And it was true. The country was still in a depression and times were hard for everybody, but especially for Uncle Edward with a new kid and all.

I opened my present. And you can bet I sat down hard when I saw what it was.

"M-Mary M-Margaret," I sputtered like a stunned cat, "I can't take this. What will you wear to Connie's party on Saturday?"

"Never mind," she said, proud as you please. "I'll wear my yellow one. The blue looks better on you."

Uncle Edward gave me a bear hug and Aunt Rosie kissed my cheek. "I wish it could be a new one, Cissy," she whispered in my ear. "Maybe next year."

Mary Margaret made me try on the dress right then. Uncle Edward whistled when he saw and made me blush. Aunt Rosie brushed my hair and fussed with the sash. You'd have thought they'd never seen me in a dress before!

It was a pretty dress—short, puffed sleeves and a big bow sash. It gaped a little in front, but Aunt Rosie said to never mind; I'd grow into it.

Mary Margaret said my bones were good. She said my brows and lashes were a natural. They looked plain old brown to me, but then I hadn't had the beauty lessons she'd had. "Wow," I thought. "I can't believe it's me, Cissy Marie Summers, primping in front of Aunt Rosie's full-length mirror in cousin Mary Margaret's best blue dress." Periwinkle blue, Aunt Rosie called it. "Periwinkle blue, to match your eyes."

"You look all grown up," Billy said and snapped the shutter on Uncle Edward's Brownie.

After I changed and hung up my new dress, Aunt Rosie said they had another surprise.

"Mrs. Freeman called," she said and smiled at Uncle Edward. "How would you like to spend the day in your old neighborhood and have lunch with Jake and his family?"

I gulped and nodded and felt my face go hot and red. "Uh, that would be fun," I stammered. I felt three kinds of stupid when I saw Mary Margaret smirk. Billy slapped his forehead and rolled his eyes to the ceiling like he expected lightning from heaven.

Outside, the wind was blowing dry and hot, so I changed into my cotton school dress and borrowed Mary Margaret's scarf to tie around my hair. Aunt Rosie wanted to ride along, so Mary Margaret said, "I'll watch Billy," then went off to paint her nails. Billy grabbed his cap from where I'd left it on the table and hustled to the sandlot on the corner. They'd started a new game by the time we drove by.

"You like Jake a lot, don't you, Cissy?" Uncle Edward asked me.

I said, "Yes, I guess I do," and Uncle Edward got all quiet for a while. Lost in thought, as Mama used to say.

Jake was waiting for us on the porch, playing ball and jacks with his little brother Tim. I almost fell down dead when I saw the way he looked, his eye all purple-hard and swollen shut. He had four stitches on his upper lip and one front tooth split up the middle. His one good eye looked like a spider in a broken web.

"Jake Freeman, you've been fighting!" I yelled right out, 'cause I was so surprised and scared to see him hurt that way. And disappointed too. I knew he couldn't kiss me this time, not with a lip like that.

Jake just grinned and slapped my arm, like it was something to be proud of. "I sure have," he said, "and I'd have beat him too if there had been just one."

Then he told how he'd been leaning on the fencepost watching that day the policemen came and took Papa away. He'd seen someone hiding in the hedge across the street. When the police car drove away, he saw Roy Cummings pop out of the bushes, brush dirt from his greasy dungarees, and walk on down the street, whistling "Yankee Doodle" and grinning like a fool.

He wanted to go after him right then and show him what he thought of snakes who snitched on other people's kin. But his mama called out for him to mind his business and come take out the garbage. When he turned around, that snake Roy Cummings had slithered off.

That was a long time ago, and he hadn't seen Roy Cummings since, but he remembered what he looked like, and one night Jake ran into Roy again. Jake told us how it went.

"I was sweeping up outside Mr. Gimble's drugstore, when Roy Cummings came staggering along, right out of Keyhole Nelson's Bar.

"Well, he didn't know me from Adam, of course, so he weaved on down the sidewalk, drunk as a skunk, and I just sort of stuck the broom out, casual-like, and sent him sprawling in the gutter."

Jake swore up and down it was an accident, but Roy didn't see it that way. He got up and took a punch at Jake, who ducked. But seeing as how Roy started it, the least Jake could do was finish, so he took a poke at Roy.

"Roy wasn't seeing too good," Jake said, "what with the whiskey in his head and gutter grime on his face, so he didn't duck. My punch knocked him back a foot or two."

Trouble was, a friend of Roy's had followed him out of Keyhole Nelson's Bar, and Jake's punch landed Roy Cummings right in this fellow's lap. By the time it all was done, the cops dragged Susi Cummings's brother Roy off to the tank, Mr. Gimble drove Jake to the doctor, and the other fellow took off for kingdom come.

Jake sure had more fun in the telling than in the doing.

Uncle Edward shook his head and said how Jake shouldn't look for trouble, and Aunt Rosie hugged his shoulders. "You poor, sweet boy," she said. "He was only defending Charles, Edward. He didn't mean to fight, did you, dear?"

Jake shook his head solemnly, but I could see the gleam in his eyes. Grandma Eva told me eyes never lie. "The eyes are the windows of the soul, Celia. If you want to know if someone is telling the truth, just look into their eyes." I looked at Jake's and knew she was right.

Mrs. Freeman said Jake's father would drive me home in time for supper. Aunt Rosie waved good-by and said, "Have fun," and Jake took me to the drugstore.

Chapter Thirty

We sat up to the counter at the soda fountain and ordered a malt. A chocolate one, big and thick, enough for two. Mr. Gimble grinned at Jake and handed us two straws. Jake grinned back and handed him a brand-new dime.

That was the best malt I've ever had, before or since. I was nervous at first 'cause I had to be so careful not to bump Jake's eye with my forehead when I bent over to take a sip, but he said I couldn't hurt him none, "a little thing like you," and he didn't hog the malt at all. In fact, he saved the last three sips for me.

Halfway to the streetcar, a block from Keyhole Nelson's Bar, we were holding hands and laughing and bending into the wind. Jake was telling me again how he'd knocked Roy Cummings into the gutter, when two men came out of the bar and started walking up the street.

Jake stopped laughing and yanked me hard into the doorway of Swift's Tobacco Shop. I banged my shin on a loose brick and started to yell. "Ouch . . . hey, what's—" But Jake clamped his hand across my mouth.

"Quiet, Cissy. It's them, Roy Cummings and the creep that gave me this eye!"

I was quiet then. I could hear voices blowing down the street on gusts on wind, just like the ghost voices in Huck Finn's cave. I couldn't understand them, though. Then the voices stopped and no one walked by so Jake peeked out and saw the heel of someone's old brown boot go sliding into the alley.

"Come on," he whispered and took his hand off my mouth. "Let's go see what those two snakes are up to."

We edged along the wall fast and quiet. When we got to the big wooden tub full of petunias in front of the movie house, the voices started up again and we ducked behind the flowers.

The alley was only two steps away, and what I heard made me sick and scared and mad as murder all at once.

"It's done, I'm telling you that. I checked on it and today's the day. He don't know nothing anyhow. All he cared about was his share of the take."

"For your sake, Roy-boy, you better be right. The boss don't like nobody running around who saw Lou Berdowski dead. The only reason you're still healthy is because you steered the heat to Summers and gave the rest of us an alibi."

My lungs shut off and my head got hot and my eyes saw yellow-black. Roy Cummings! He knew who killed Lou Berdowski. He knew and blamed Papa on purpose so the others could go free.

Later, Jake told me how they talked about my papa helping to take money from the bank and acting too high-handed, wanting more than his fair share. He and Lou Berdowski had gotten into an argument and Papa told him to hand over his share or else. But next day Roy Cummings's friend and another man killed Lou Berdowski for his share, and Roy Cummings come along and said how he could see to it that my papa took the rap and no one would be the wiser. And they said he'd better or he would be dead too.

I don't remember any of that. I just remember seeing yellow-black, then the pink and white petunias and the thick green

Coke bottle someone had stuck in the planter.

I grabbed that bottle by the neck and ran. Jake said I was down the sidewalk to the alley before he could even blink. I hauled back with my pitching arm, focused on the back of Roy Cummings's head and let the bottle fly.

It was a good throw. Right on target. It would have smashed Roy Cummings's head wide open if it hadn't been a gust of wind came down the alley and set the bottle down an inch too soon. It smacked into his shoulder hard and sent him spinning. Then Jake grabbed my arm and we were gone.

We ran and ran, till my chest burned like a red-hot coal. I tripped once and kicked off my shoes. Jake never let go of me, not once, and he knew where we were going.

The police station was just four blocks away. If it had been much more than that, I'd have died for sure. The sergeant at the desk said how we looked like we'd been wrestling tigers.

We told our story and they sent someone to look, but there was no sign of Roy Cummings or the other man. The bottle was there, and a speck or two of blood, so I guess they had to believe us. Some of it anyway. I think they thought how it must have been Jake who threw the bottle. It was him they scolded and told we should never have been there in the first place; spying on criminals could get us killed.

"This is police business," they said and put us in a car. A policeman drove us home to Jake's.

Mrs. Freeman said she about fainted when she saw the police car pull up front with me and Jake in back. Mr. Freeman went for his razor strap but put it back when the policeman told him how it was.

After he drove me home, Mr. Freeman walked me to the door and asked would I like him to come in and tell Uncle Edward what happened. I said, "Yes, please." I felt all shaky cold inside, even though the thermometer in Aunt Rosie's kitchen window said eighty-five degrees.

Aunt Rosie hustled me right off to the bath and made me crawl in for a soak. I couldn't even tell Jake good-by. When I got out, Mary Margaret handed me a note from Jake and said, "Supper's ready."

I wasn't the least bit hungry. My stomach felt like it wanted to get rid of the malt I'd had with Jake. I started to tell her, "No thanks," but remembered Aunt Rosie had made a special dinner for my birthday and I should at least sit at the table.

Billy followed me to the room I shared with Mary Margaret. "Did you really murder someone with a bottle?" he whispered, grinning from ear to ear and faking pitches with his throwing arm.

I didn't answer. Just shut the door and opened up Jake's note. I guess that was pretty rude, but I didn't want to talk about it then.

The note said, "Don't worry, Cissy, everything will be all right. See you soon. Love, Jake."

I didn't know if everything would be all right or not, but I read the "Love, Jake" part three times, then folded the note real small and put it in the bottom of my underwear drawer.

My dress was dirty from cutting through the alley behind Mr. Gimble's store to get to the police station. The new blue one was hanging in the closet along with several others. I wanted to save it for Sunday best, but Aunt Rosie had said, "Fourteen is a special birthday, Cissy," so I put it on and went down to supper.

Aunt Rosie had cooked roast beef and mashed potatoes, my favorites, but I couldn't swallow much and she said to never mind. "We'll save the cake for tomorrow, Cissy. You'll feel better then."

Chapter
Thirty-one

None of us knew Papa's dying would be on the news. Like Uncle Edward said later, he never would have turned on the radio if he'd known. I told him never mind. It wouldn't change things one bit. Papa would still be dead and I would have known about it sooner or later.

But Uncle Edward did turn on the radio right after supper. He'd already called the warden at the prison to tell what Roy had said, but the warden wasn't there and the person who answered said they'd give him the message.

It was already too late.

"Charles Wayne Summers died today in the electric chair. He was convicted of murder in the death of Lou Berdowski, one of the area's most prominent union leaders ..." The radio blurted it all right out. And I heard Roy Cummings say, "It's done. Today's the day," just like he was still standing in the alley, with me and Jake hiding behind the petunias.

I couldn't believe it. I just couldn't. I ran upstairs, hung my new blue dress in the back of Mary Margaret's closet, and crawled in after it. I wanted to stay there forever in the cool dark, in just my shift and petticoat, curled up in the corner with a wheel from Mary Margaret's roller skate poking my back. The feel of that wheel reminded me I was alive.

I was alive, but Papa wasn't.

I laid my head against the rough closet wall. I wished there was a button I could push, a secret panel that would open in the wall. I'd tumble through into a world of make-believe, like Alice down the rabbit hole, and not be real for a while. Real hurts. Sometimes, being real hurts real bad.

After a while I heard Aunt Rosie and Uncle Edward talking in the hall. I tried to cover my ears, but I'd finally had enough of Mary Margaret's roller skate and I had to move.

"For goodness sake, go find her, Rose. I had no idea she was standing there. I would never have turned on that blamed radio if I had known they were going to broadcast it all over the city!" Uncle Edward sounded close to tears.

I had to strain to hear Aunt Rosie's answer. "Leave her be, Edward. Let the poor child grieve. She's kept her feelings bottled up too long; it's about time she let some of them out. I'll go to her later."

I could almost see her touch his arm the way she does when he's close enough. They're always touching, those two. Like Papa and Mama way back when I was nine or ten, before the trouble came.

"Lord love that child. We should have told her, Rose," Uncle Edward said then. "We should have told her when we first found out.

"I'm going into our room to pray."

* * *

It's cold and dark at midnight, even here in sunny California. I stayed in the closet and sobbed until I felt goose bumps creeping up and down my arms. I couldn't cry anymore, so I crawled out into the room and slipped into my nightgown quiet as I could.

Mary Margaret was asleep on her side, finger-curls spread

behind her on the pillow like a pleated fan we saw at the fair. Her hands were folded underneath her cheek like she'd been praying when she fell asleep. Her face looked so peaceful, like she didn't have a care. I wondered if she'd been praying for me.

I had to use the facilities real bad. I tiptoed down the hall, but Aunt Rosie must have heard, 'cause when I got back to bed she was waiting with a cup of hot cocoa and a slice of bread spread with butter and honey the way I like it. I couldn't eat it, though.

I took a sip of cocoa to please her, but I'd have rather had a sip of Papa's whiskey. Then I'd be all warm inside. And fuzzy in the head, like floating in a dream where nothing's real.

Aunt Rosie sat on my bed a long time. She rubbed my back and let me cry.

I remembered when Bruno Richard Hauptmann was electrocuted back in April for killing Mr. Lindbergh's baby. I had asked God if it would hurt to die that way and wondered if Mr. Hauptmann felt sorry for what he'd done.

"It's not fair!" I blurted out and threw my pillow on the floor. "Papa didn't kill no one. He didn't!"

Mary Margaret groaned and rolled over on her bed to face the wall. Aunt Rosie didn't scold or tell me, "*Anyone,* not *no one,* Cissy." She just sighed and brushed the hair off my forehead like Mama used to do when I was little and had a fever. "Only God knows, sweetheart," she whispered from the darkness.

That made me mad. "Where is God?" I asked Aunt Rosie. "Miss Goodwin said he'd never leave me, but he's sure not here right now. Where is God when it hurts so bad you want to kick and scream and hit somebody really hard?"

Aunt Rosie let me carry on awhile, about Papa being dead and Mama gone, and God taking Krista up to heaven when she wasn't old enough to go. I blubbered how I wanted to tell Chuckie a story and cuddle Baby Grace.

She didn't stop me till I got to Susi Cummings's brother Roy. I'd worked up to a full boil by then.

"It was him that did it!" Trying to whisper mad was hard. "That dirty snake Roy Cummings killed that Lou Berdowski and blamed it on my papa just for spite."

Aunt Rosie picked up my pillow and stuffed it back behind my head. "Hush now, child," she said. "You don't know he did any such thing! You're accusing him like he accused your papa. Don't you know that's just as bad?"

I lay back on my pillow. I didn't like it, but I knew she was right. From what Roy said, he'd only seen the killing, not done it himself. But he'd still accused Papa and that was just the same as murder. It was Roy Cummings who deserved to die!

I hadn't liked Roy even back in Pike. Something about him made me feel sick inside, but my conscience wouldn't let me be.

"Oh, Aunt Rosie," I sighed, leaning up on my elbow and smoothing the crinkled skin across the back of her hand. "Did God go away because he knows how much I hate Susi's brother Roy?"

Aunt Rosie laughed. "Land, child, what am I to do with you?" She shook her head, then pressed her hand against my cheek. "God didn't leave you, Cissy. You just can't feel him right now because your heart's so full of grief."

She pulled the covers to my chin. "God didn't leave your papa either, rest his soul." She closed her eyes a minute and I felt bad because I knew it was really late and she was tired and had to go to choir tomorrow at church. But I just had to know.

"Why did Papa take the money, Aunt Rosie? Why didn't he tell me about you and Uncle Edward after Mama went away?"

Aunt Rosie sighed. A big deep sigh that seemed to come clear up from her toes—a soul sigh, Grandma Eva used to call it.

"Lord knows Charles never meant to hurt anyone, Cissy. Especially not you and your mama or the little ones. He was

—157—

just mixed up, is all. He wanted so much for you all to be happy, he thought he had to take matters on himself instead of trusting God to see you through the hard times."

"Is Papa in heaven?" I felt cold all over. I was there when Papa accepted Jesus as Savior, but he'd done some awful things since then and I wasn't sure what God would do about that.

Aunt Rosie sat still and quiet for a long time. When she looked at me, I could see her cheeks were wet.

"We have to trust, sweetheart," she whispered. "We have to trust your papa's soul to God."

She wiped her eyes with a corner of the bedspread, picked up the cup of cold cocoa and stood beside the bed.

"Would you like to see your mama tomorrow, Cissy?" she asked right out of the clear blue.

I nodded yes. My throat felt like I'd swallowed a hen egg whole.

"Good," she said. "We'll go right after supper. Can you sleep now?"

I nodded yes again and closed my eyes to show her, and I guess I didn't move till morning.

C h a p t e r
T h i r t y - t w o

When I woke up, I knew I'd had the dream. I remembered it like it was real. Only this time there was more to it than usual, and all the parts fit together like pieces of the jigsaw puzzle we've been working on all summer. The puzzle's set up on one end of the table in the dining room, and every time someone walks by they try to find a piece that fits. Every day the picture gets clearer and clearer. It won't be long until we see the whole thing.

I opened my eyes and saw sunlight streaming through the window, shining right on Mary Margaret's curls. I heard the whippoorwill call from the eucalyptus tree outside my window, and Tarzan was purring on the pillow by my ear. The warm doughy smell of pancakes frying in the kitchen told me Aunt Rosie was already up.

My heart still pounded from the dream. I felt like I'd been running for hours, chased by something with hot breath and evil, gleaming eyes and a face that looked like Susi Cummings's brother Roy.

I had to find out if the dream was real, so I brushed my teeth, pulled on Billy's hand-me-down jeans, and tiptoed down the hallway.

Colby was still asleep, curled up in front of Billy's bedroom door. He opened one brown eye and yawned, but let me pass without a whine.

The carpet on the stairs felt rough under my bare feet, but it was too late to go back for slippers. I stepped over the third stair from the bottom so it wouldn't squeak and made it out the front door with no one the wiser.

My diary had been in the box Jake brought, with Tarzan and Krista's Cecilia doll. I kept it under the pile of bricks behind the garage, away from Mary Margaret's prying eyes and Billy's snoopy nose. It was quiet there. Uncle Edward had let the bushes grow up, and Billy always forgot to mow the grass. "Can't see it anyway," he would mutter when Uncle Edward found out and made him do it over. But that didn't happen much and the grass stayed long and soft, a perfect place to read and think and write.

I grabbed an old dead twig and poked at the bricks. Sure enough, three small brown spiders scurried out, along with one that could have been a widow, but I didn't get close enough to look. When I was sure there were no more insects, I moved the bottom brick and pulled my diary from its hiding place. Looking around, I could see that the back of the garage was still in the shade; I figured I had about half an hour before Mary Margaret would wake up enough to wonder where I was.

Like I told Mama later, it's funny how something that's so much a part of you can still hold secrets. Things I wrote myself, but never understood until today. Like that Fourth of July before I turned eleven and Papa lost his job. Before we found out Mama was going to have another baby.

All the diary said was, "Susi Cummings and I took Krista to the carnival today. Boy did we have fun, but Krista got sick on the Spinner and threw up all over Susi's lap and we had to bring her home early."

Chapter Thirty-two

It was enough to make me remember.

They had set up the carnival in the empty lot behind the Methodist church. Papa said we probably couldn't go because it cost too much and it was just a bunch of nonsense anyway. Mama had been cross all morning, snapping the dish towel extra hard and flipping Krista's lip for sassing when all Krista wanted was a cookie.

After Papa went to work, Susi Cummings and I decided to take our roller hoops outside where we'd be out of Mama's way. We were chasing them round and round the big old maple tree when Susi's brother Roy came by with our copy of the *Pike Review.* He wouldn't give it to me, though. He held it out of reach and marched it right up to the porch. Mama met him at the door.

Next thing I knew he was in the kitchen stirring sugar into Papa's coffee mug, laughing and smiling to beat the band. Mama was laughing too, sitting there across from him, all pink and pretty in her satin robe. That's when Roy handed me and Susi a dollar each and said, "Take Krista to the carnival."

Susi and I both let out a whoop. She grabbed the money and I grabbed Krista's shoes.

"Be good now, hear?" Mama smiled as we dragged Krista out the door. "Be good, and keep ahold of Krista's hand."

Roy Cummings was just leaving when we brought Krista home.

I put the diary between the bricks and snuck back into the house.

At breakfast they all treated me like one of Mama's fancy china plates. Mary Margaret poured my glass of milk before her own. Billy scooped Tarzan off my chair and held the back till I sat down.

Aunt Rosie put her hand against my face. "You look flushed, sweetheart. Are you sure you don't want to stay in bed today?

I have to sing, but Mary Margaret could—"

"Oh, no," I interrupted her, "I feel fine!" I flashed my brightest smile to fool them.

Uncle Edward touched my hand and said, "Don't worry, Cissy, the police will catch up with Roy Cummings and his lowlife friends."

"That's right." Aunt Rosie's voice squeaked as she reached across the table and poured the last of the syrup on my pancakes. "And I'm sure you'll feel much better after you see your mama today."

Billy stared at my plate, then at the empty syrup bottle. He started to say something, but caught Mary Margaret's glare and reached for the jelly jar instead.

Aunt Rosie shook her head and looked at Uncle Edward. "It's been much too long. I don't know why we didn't take her before."

Uncle Edward said something back, but I didn't pay much attention. I was too relieved that Aunt Rosie had remembered her promise.

Later, in the morning sermon, Pastor Stewart preached on Jacob. Jacob had to go on a long journey, away from all his family. He was alone in the wilderness and probably afraid. Jacob fell asleep and dreamed about a ladder going up to heaven. God was at the top of the ladder and said to Jacob, "I am with thee and will keep thee in all places."

I could hear Miss Goodwin saying clear as yesterday, "God will never leave you, Cissy."

The sermon went on and on. Jacob went to live with his uncle and fell in love and had to work twice as long as he was supposed to, which wasn't fair, but he did it anyway and wound up with two wives and lots of children, and then they all ran away. He was going to find his brother, but had some trouble and had to wrestle with an angel.

While Jacob wrestled with the angel, I wrestled with the Lord, right there in the third pew from the front, sitting next to Mary Margaret and listening to Mr. Bristol snore.

What had happened to me in the last few years wasn't fair, but God had led me through the wilderness too, and helped me out of trouble, and given me a family who loved me. If he could do all that for me, he could take care of Mama too, and Papa's soul to boot.

When the sermon ended and we all filed out the door, I shook the pastor's hand, smiled a real smile, and looked him in the eye.

Chapter
Thirty-three

I almost changed my mind when we got to the hospital. The building was old, with red-brick walls that showed cracks where the mortar had crumbled. The trees and shrubs were neat and trimmed—Grandma Eva would have liked that—and the lawn was green. Too green. Cemetery green. All the windows above the first floor had thick white bars and wire where the glass should be.

A huge brown lady in a white uniform waved a clipboard at us and blocked our way. "This girl is much too young," she huffed. "The rules say you have to be sixteen."

Uncle Edward disappeared into a glass-walled office where an older man in a dark blue suit peered out at us over wire-rimmed spectacles. The man smiled and shook Uncle Edward's hand.

I held my breath.

It wasn't but a minute and Uncle Edward came back, a ring of keys in one hand and a piece of paper in the other.

The guard read the note and shook her head, then led us down the hall and up two flights of stairs.

The halls smelled sour and strong, worse than Papa's whiskey. I hurried after Uncle Edward, careful not to touch the walls or any of the wooden chairs that sat beside some of the bolted doors.

The guard stopped at the last door on the third floor. Before she turned the lock, she looked at me hard. "Your mother won't know you," she warned. "Mrs. Summers never talks to anyone."

But she was wrong. Mama knew me the minute I walked into the room. I know because she looked me right in the eye and said, "Your papa didn't do it, Cissy. Charles was a lot of things, but he was not a murderer."

I thought the guard was going to faint. Uncle Edward took her by the arm and left the room. Aunt Rosie touched my hand, then walked out too.

Mama nodded and went all quiet again. I could see her slipping back into the world inside her head. But I could get her back. I knew that, sure as I was standing there.

* * *

I can see us both reflected in the dressing-table mirror. Mama and me. She's sitting behind me, on the edge of the bed. Looks so peaceful-calm, holding Papa's letter up close to her chest, a soft, sweet smile on her lips. She's talking to him again.

She watches me take the letter from the table by her bed, but only smiles when I ask, "Can I read it?" I take her smile for a yes, and pull it from the envelope.

The envelope is gray. The paper too. Everything in prison must be gray. Imagine never seeing any colors!

The date is August 27, 1936. Just a week ago. Papa knew he was going to die, but he wasn't scared.

"I've made my peace with God," the letter says. "Death will mean freedom for me. Not because I killed another man—you and I both know that, Lynetta. But I killed our family, sure as I'm sitting in this prison cell.

"I accept the blame for all of it, you know. If I had been a better husband, you would not have turned to someone else. We

made mistakes, you and I, and the most that we can offer each
other is forgiveness."

So, Papa knew.

Mama looks younger than me today. Her skin's so smooth
and pretty. Even without any lipstick or rouge she could always
make Papa's head turn.

I guess I do look older than fourteen in cousin Mary Margaret's best blue dress. Periwinkle blue to match my eyes. Mama's eyes.

I have Mama's forehead too. And her heart-shaped face and
cork-stub nose plastered with a million freckles. Papa always
said it would take a year from Tuesday to count the freckles on
Mama's nose. But then he'd say, "I'd like to try," and Mama's
cheeks would turn pink-red. "Land, Charles," she'd say, "don't
take on so in front of the children!"

My hair's not like Mama's, though. It's lighter, almost blonde.
I used to sneak into Mama's room in Pike and sit in front of
the brass frame mirror and wonder how my hair would look
piled up all nice and high on top of my head. Fastened with
jeweled combs or maybe a soft, blue velvet ribbon. But then
Jimmy Wilson would come knocking and ask was I ready to
go to school, and hurry 'cause it's half past seven and we would
be late for sure, and he wasn't going to waste any more time
waiting on some mamby-pamby girl.

He could sure yank my hair hard, that Jimmy Wilson.

Mama's rocking now and singing "Lu La Baby Li." I wonder
if it's that baby in heaven or Baby Grace she's singing to.

Papa's with that baby now, and Krista and Grandma Eva.
I'm sure of it. Didn't the letter say he'd made his peace with
God? Papa's with Mama too. Maybe more than he ever was.

Mama can hear me, I know she can. She looks all lost and
lonely, hiding there inside her head, but her eyes are sharp as
a stepped-on tack.

I'd like to tell her how sad I feel for her and Papa, and how Aunt Rosie says we'll all be together again in heaven someday. I'd like to say, "I forgive you, Mama, for leaving me alone." But that's not why I came.

"Look in the mirror, Mama. See how much I've grown? I've learned a lot this year. Billy taught me to play baseball, and Mary Margaret taught me how to put on lipstick and curl my hair. Aunt Rosie and Uncle Edward taught me things about God and prayer and forgiveness and what it really means to love.

"Are you listening, Mama? 'Cause it's important. I know the truth, you see. I know about you and Roy Cummings and what you did the day of the carnival. I know why he left Pike in such a hurry. I know why Papa started drinking again, and stole money from the bank, and why we moved to California.

"It's a funny thing about the truth: you can run from it and try to hide, and it will catch you every time. But if you turn and look it in the eye—stare it down—you realize it can't hurt you anymore. Then you're free, Mama, do you understand? Then you're really free."

Epilogue

That day at Mama's bedside was a turning point for me. I realized that in spite of everything I was happier than I'd been in a long time. It felt good to know I'd forgiven Mama for what she'd done with Roy and her part in all that happened afterward. I could tell by the way she looked at me that we understood each other.

I still had a lot to learn about God's working in the human heart, but I realized that Mama would have to face the truth and deal with it in her own way.

As for Papa, I was relieved to know that he'd renewed his faith in God. He had died only the day before, but had been lost to us for over a year. It was time to forgive him too.

That day, looking in the mirror, watching Mama smile and nod her head, I felt a sense of freedom, an exquisite feeling of anticipation that something wonderful was about to happen.

Oh, I knew it wasn't over, not the grieving anyway. But I was fourteen years old. I had my whole life ahead of me. My childhood was a time to keep—but safely locked away, like my diary and my new blue dress. I would bring it out and look at it once in a while, and maybe someday the hurting would stop. Maybe someday I'd learn to forget.